# BORDERLAND

## Pamela Beason

**WildWing Press**
**Bellingham, Washington, USA**

# Copyright Page

This is a work of fiction. Names, characters, places, and incidents are products of the author's imagination or are used fictitiously and are not to be construed as real. Although many of the locations mentioned in this book are real, details have been changed and other places invented for the sake of the story. Any semblance to actual events, locales, organizations, or persons, living or dead, is entirely coincidental.

WILDWING PRESS
3301 Brandywine Court
Bellingham, Washington 98226

# 1

The jaguar stood on his hind legs, his massive front paws stretched high against the metal mesh of the tall fence panel. The regal cat's nose was raised, and the focus of his gaze was the coil of concertina wire at the top of the wall, ten feet above his head.

In the photo, taken at a three-quarter angle, the jaguar's yearning to get beyond that wall was so painful it brought tears to Sam's eyes. She swiveled her desk chair away from her laptop to glare at Jade Silva's empty bed. Picking up her mug of cooling coffee, she took a sip. Last night the young photographer had hinted that she'd made connections that put her on the trail of a rare jaguar in Arizona's southeastern mountains, and Sam had intended to tag along with her. However, in the fifteen days they'd shared a room as well as their love of animals, Sam learned that not only did Jade never hang up any article of clothing, she could also be as stealthy as an owl when she was stalking the perfect photo. Sometime during the night, Jade had annoyingly slipped out without waking Sam.

At first, Sam wondered why her roommate would have emailed her a black photo. Curious about why the photo was so dark, she made a copy of the file and set to work on changing the lighting. It was clear now that Jade had taken the photo somewhere along the border wall in the pre-dawn hours, and maybe that was why Jade had emailed the image to Sam. Jade Silva's nature photos sold for thousands in Santa Fe. Part of their allure was that Jade guaranteed they were unretouched; she refused to manipulate any picture she shot. Sam was the woman with the Photoshop skills.

Did Jade intend to give her the photo? Sam swung back to concentrate on the laptop screen again. She wanted this picture so badly she could taste it. "Powerful" was the best adjective she could think of to describe the image.

Tweaking the lighting a bit more, she brought out soft colors as they would be in early dawn. The barren ground at the jaguar's feet was deep grey-beige powder, crisscrossed with dozens of tire tracks between the photographer and the cat. The heavy mesh under the jaguar's outstretched front paws was rust-orange. A formerly portable helicopter landing mat, Sam had been told, a leftover from the Vietnam era. Many of these military surplus items had been repurposed as panels for the patchwork barrier that was the border wall between the United States and Mexico. The shiny concertina wire looping along the top was an ominous recent addition.

Viewed through the heavy steel mesh, the scenery on the other side of the wall, the Mexican side, was green and lush as far as the eye could see, the vegetation so thick it was hard to imagine that anyone could walk through it. The contrast of that verdant countryside with the barren foreground on the US side was stark. The northern side showed only sand, gravel, tumbleweeds, and tire tracks.

Saving her work on both the laptop and a thumb drive, Sam groaned with frustration at her roommate's absence. Where was Jade? She needed this photo. It was perfect; it was important. Photos of deer, pronghorns, coyotes, and even horned toads halted at the border wall had made the covers of conservation magazines and the home pages of environmental websites, but the resulting outrage rarely radiated beyond the confines of the conservation groups. This image could inspire hundreds of thousands of wildlife lovers and ecologists and border-wall critics to rise up in a green tsunami. When a video of a javelina sow with five tiny babies trying futilely to find a way through the border wall trended on YouTube a few months ago, the resulting protests had succeeded in halting construction for several weeks.

Two jaguars had been sighted in Arizona in recent years, and the presence of each was widely celebrated across the state, with photos in every newspaper. Native American tribes in Arizona, New Mexico, and Texas had revived their traditional ceremonies to welcome the big cats back to their northernmost range.

Then, several months ago, the hide of one of those jaguars, nicknamed El Jefe, had appeared on eBay. The authorities were supposedly investigating, but whoever had been in possession of the hide remained anonymous as well as silent about how they'd come to acquire the skin of that magnificent cat. To the sorrow and outrage of wildlife lovers, these days both federal and state governments largely ignored the Endangered Species Act.

So now, as far as anyone knew, there was only one wild jaguar left in Arizona. This photo would definitely cause the biggest uproar yet. Sam wanted that attention. The wall may have been intended to keep migrants out, but it was only slowing them down.

However, the barricade was extremely successful in preventing the migration of wildlife. Fatally successful, and would be more so each year as more of the wall was completed according to plan. The proof was on Sam's computer screen right now, showing that the lone jaguar in Arizona was in solitary confinement, imprisoned in the United States.

As dawn peeked over the cliffs, the local birds enthusiastically greeted the sun. A canyon wren trilled its sweet song from a tree not far away, then the melody was drowned out by the closer hammering of a woodpecker. Sam had the day off, and she was looking forward to exploring Cave Creek Canyon and climbing one of the local peaks. But first, she desperately wanted to talk to her roommate.

Jade had taken hundreds of photos in the time they'd shared a room. Although she'd shown Sam many of them and even allowed Sam to use a few of the ones she didn't want to keep, Jade had never sent her a picture via email before. Why now, and why just that one photo? Because Jade considered it a rare treasure, or because she considered the image a throwaway?

No doubt the photographer would return with stunning shots of rare birds, the sparkle of early morning sun on a trickle of water down a cliffside, or a prize photo of a female bobcat carrying her kitten in her mouth. And probably, more shots of that jaguar. Unbelievable, that Jade had driven all the way south to the border wall this morning. She must have had a tip about where that jaguar might be headed.

A jaguar, in Arizona! The magnificent cats, the largest felines in the western hemisphere, had once roamed from the US Southwest to the jungles of South America. Now, they were as rare as red wolves north of the border. Not only was Sam dying to see a jaguar in the wild, but she could learn a lot from a professional photographer like Jade Silva. Sam's pictures were good enough to appear in online blogs and the occasional print magazine, but Jade's photos were *art*. And while Sam's skills were good enough to earn her repeat assignments, the gaps between contracts could be as vast as the Arizona desert.

Sighing, she filled her travel coffeemaker with fresh water

and grounds, and brewed a second cup. Then, with steaming mug and camera in hand, Sam wandered out into the early morning light of the Southwestern Research Station. Bird-watchers slipped silently through the trees like wandering ghosts, binoculars swinging from their necks, occasionally signaling to their comrades when they'd spotted a different avian species.

The variety of apparel worn by the early-morning explorers made it easy to discern where they were from. Those visitors from warm climates wore puffy jackets or fleece in the brisk dawn air at the 5400-foot elevation; those from cooler home territories, like Sam, sported only a windbreaker or flannel shirt. She'd learned that once the sun moved fully above the surrounding mountains, fifty degrees would quickly change to seventy or higher in the thin dry air. This was early May. It already felt like summer to Sam's internal thermostat.

Many of the birders were older than Sam, but they didn't seem as affected by the altitude. As a resident of the sea-level Pacific Northwest coast, her breathing was surprisingly challenged here; it was all she could do not to pant audibly when strolling from one building to another. Although she frequently hiked to the high peaks of the North Cascades, she didn't live in this thin air every day.

She perched on a bench among the hummingbird feeders, sipping her coffee. Setting her cell phone camera on rapid-fire mode, she aimed it at the closest feeder and snapped multiple shots as two rufous males and a magnificent hummingbird chased each other from the nectar. Only two gray-green Annas amicably shared the feeder. Females, obviously.

"Sam." The bench shifted as Beverly Mayer lowered her substantial weight onto the other end of the bench.

"Morning," Sam murmured.

In a more formal environment, Bev would probably be

called the chef, but here the volunteers knew her as The Boss. Even before dawn, she was busy mixing or chopping or baking. Sam had never beat Bev to the kitchen in the morning or left when Bev was not there in the evening. She wondered when the woman slept. It was rare to see her outside the dining hall like this.

"Have you seen Jade?" Bev asked.

Both Sam and Jade had signed up as volunteers. Sam had been unable to pass up this incredible deal; only twenty-four hours of work per week in exchange for six weeks of room and board. While Jade had come to explore the forested canyons and rocky cliffs and take her nature photographs, Sam was here to study the ecology of the Sky Islands, as the isolated clusters of steep mountains that abruptly rose from the surrounding desert floor were called.

When not weed-whacking or washing dishes or cleaning the bathrooms, the volunteers' time was their own. Both Jade and Sam hiked, sometimes together, more often apart, Jade taking photos and Sam gathering notes and pictures for the articles she'd promised to four different conservation groups.

"Jade's on kitchen duty as of"— Bev raised her left wrist and checked her watch— "five minutes ago. We have sixty-eight to feed this morning."

"Did you—"

"I knocked on your door," Bev responded to Sam's unfinished question. "Then I peeked in. Nobody home. Did Jade go walkabout again?"

Sam couldn't wait to go walkabout herself. The trail in Cave Creek Canyon beckoned her to explore it all the way to the cliff top today. Taking another sip of coffee, she watched a black-chinned hummingbird flash its purple neck feathers before lighting on the feeder. With luck, she might see an elegant trogon along that trail before noon; some of the visiting birders had reported seeing those exotic long-tailed avian beauties in that area.

She attempted to reassure Bev. "I'm sure Jade will show up in a minute or two."

"Until she does . . .," Bev let the suggestion hang in the air as she stood up, rocking the bench. The hummers zipped away from the closest feeder.

After swilling the last of her coffee, Sam exhaled heavily. "Coming."

Jade was going to owe her. Again.

But Sam was willing to take Jade's shifts for days to come if it meant that jaguar photo was hers.

# 2

It was one thirty in the afternoon by the time Sam finished chopping and stirring and supplying the serving line at breakfast and lunch, then washing dishes and scrubbing tables after both meals. While her hands were occupied, her imagination invented way too many scenarios that might have happened to Jade—car accident, hiking accident, shot while trespassing, arrested while trespassing, arrested by the US Border Patrol, shot or kidnapped by militia types loaded with surplus testosterone and high-powered weapons, shot or kidnapped by drug runners with the same.

The possibilities were awful and endless.

On the other hand, Sam couldn't help but grit her teeth in annoyance as the day slipped by while she fulfilled all her roommate's duties. She was really going to be pissed if Jade was gleefully snapping photos of the big cat washing its beautiful orange and black-rosetted face with a curled paw like a tame tabby. Although Sam had to admit that if *she'd* somehow stumbled upon a jaguar, only the threat of death could have kept her from tracking that awe-inspiring cat for as long as she possibly could.

Like Sam, Jade had an SUV, but unlike Sam's 2007 faded blue well-worn RAV4, Jade's deep-red hybrid Honda CR-V was so new that its hubcaps were still shiny. The thing probably got nearly twice the gas mileage that Sam's did. Her roommate kept extra water, extra food, extra clothes, and even a sleeping bag in her SUV so that if the conditions along any route promised a perfect photograph only hours away, Jade could stay until she captured it. The sticker on the back bumper, Wild Girl, perfectly described the vehicle's owner.

According to Sam's email, the jaguar photo had been sent at 5:16 a.m. By now, Jade could have driven all the way west to Nogales or even Organ Pipe Cactus National Monument, or east to half of New Mexico. Or had she followed that jaguar back into the local mountains? Maybe right now she was trailing that lithe cat as it slipped down a canyon trail, its spotted hide blending into the dappled shadows.

"You've been scrubbing that same spot for five minutes," Bev loudly stated, jogging Sam out of her mental meanderings.

Sam stared at the corner of the dining table under her cleaning cloth.

Bev folded her arms across her chest like a drill sergeant. "Dismissed, soldier." Then she grinned. "Thanks for filling in for Jade. She owes you plenty."

"Got that right." Hanging her wet cleaning rag on the drying rack, Sam headed back to the dormitory. The day wasn't completely lost. She still had plenty of sunlight to hunt down that elegant trogon, and maybe Jade had returned, or sent another image in email, or at least an explanation of her vanishing act. While there was no cell phone coverage at the station, there was internet. But she was met with disappointment when she opened the door. Jade's bed remained untouched, the sheets and blanket still thrown back as she had left them.

Sam fired up her laptop while she stuffed her daypack with snacks, sunscreen, binoculars, and her new cell phone, which had good enough zoom that it was doing double duty as her camera on this trip. Turning, she again implored the empty space. "Jade, where are you?"

One long raven hair undulated across the plain white pillowcase. As Sam twisted her own fine silver-blond tresses into her typical French braid for hiking, she reflected that she'd always wanted hair like Jade's, black with russet highlights, full and dark and wavy. Jade had the same gorgeous mane as Sam's foster-child friend Maya Velasquez. While Jade's hung halfway down her back, Maya kept hers short and spiked with gel, wanting to project a tough image at age nineteen. At least now the girl had let her hair go from an unnatural purple-red back to its original color, the same lustrous ebony as Jade's.

When Sam first reported for volunteer duty at the station, her assigned roommate had been out taking photos. Sam had shifted the mound of clothing and personal items from the bare mattress on her side of the room to the narrow, rumpled bed on the other side. Alone in the room, she'd snooped a bit, noting that Jade's desk held no computer. Scattered across the desktop were five colorful rocks that might have been some sort of valuable gems or minerals in the rough, a small wood carving of a pronghorn, and another of a wild boar. The tiny figurines were amazingly intricate, with eyes and whiskers and hollowed-out ears. The pronghorn wore a surprised expression, while the boar appeared belligerently poised to gore a victim.

Back in Bellingham, her young friend Maya had a carving in the same style: an intricate wolf howling at the moon, complete with detailed swirls of fur, sharply pointed ears, and even a delicate tongue inside its open mouth. Maya carried that carving everywhere. She'd even kept it in her tent when she camped in Sam's backyard.

When she first learned that she'd have another volunteer

as a roommate at the station, Sam had experienced a pang of anxiety. She shared her home with Blake, but they each had a private bedroom and bathroom. Here, she'd be sharing a small dorm room with a stranger. She feared that six weeks could feel like an eternity if she were paired with a religious type seeking to make a convert or a woman who constantly wanted to show Sam the latest Facebook photos of her grandchildren. When the director told her that she'd be rooming with Jade Silva, a professional wildlife photographer, Sam had been greatly relieved. She'd looked forward to meeting a kindred spirit.

Sam had been at her laptop after she'd arrived, typing up notes about the unique qualities of the Southwestern Research Station when Jade finally strode into their dorm room after dark, a daypack slung over her shoulder and her sunglasses pushed to the top of her head.

She'd casually waved a hand in the air. "Hey, I'm Jade."

Sam's jaw had dropped. Although she was older, Jade was the spitting image of Maya. Sam couldn't help staring at her new roommate's deeply-lashed, slightly slanted, dark-brown eyes, her thick black hair, her distinctive bow-shaped mouth.

"Are you okay?" A cautious smile played across Jade's lips as she shoved aside the tangle of clothes and perched on her bed, dropping her pack on the floor in front of her feet.

Chagrin set Sam's cheeks on fire. She lowered her gaze to the floor for a second before meeting Jade's eyes again. Then she stood up and offered a hand. "Sorry. I'm Sam." Then, dropping back into her chair, she explained, "Well, my name's Summer Westin, really, but I go by Sam. Did you know you have a doppelganger?"

"A doppelganger? Yikes." Jade glanced down at her chest and arms. "Is that some kind of spider?"

Sam chuckled. "It means a double. I have a young friend

named Maya back home who looks just like you. And I do mean *just* like you."

"Oh, thank God. I don't like creepy-crawlies. And speaking of that, there are scorpions here. They're tiny, but you probably don't want to walk around barefoot." The photographer nodded at Sam's bare feet.

"Good to know." Sam searched the room for her flip-flops. There they were, on the bottom shelf of her storage area.

Abruptly, Jade perked up, her eyes suddenly intense. "Wait a minute. Did you say Maya? Like the ancient people in Mexico?"

Sam nodded.

"Where's 'back home'?"

"Bellingham, Washington. Close to the Canadian border, about two hours drive north of Seattle."

"Is this Maya"—Jade's gaze shifted toward the ceiling as she considered— "around twenty years old?"

"How'd you know?" Sam was stunned. "Maya Velasquez will be twenty on her next birthday."

"I can't believe this." The bed frame creaked as Jade leaned forward. "Do you have a photo of Maya?"

Pulling her cell phone from her bedside table, Sam thumbed through it. The best image she could find was a shot from the Wilderness Quest trip she'd led last fall. Maya had been one of two youth counselors along on the expedition with six troubled teens. After enlarging the photo, Sam held out the phone, her fingertip on Maya, who stood arm in arm with two of the client kids.

Jade leaped up from the bed, pulled the phone from Sam's hand, then stared at the image for a long time. "Oh. My. God." Sucking in a breath, she traced a fingertip over her own cupid's bow mouth, then slowly exhaled. Finally, she murmured, "Maya. Wow."

Sam raised an eyebrow.

Jade chuckled at Sam's perplexed expression. "Talk about synchronicity. I can't believe it. It's hard to take in, but I think Maya might actually be my half sister." Then she shook her head and ran her fingers through her long black hair. "I can't believe it," she repeated. "Maya is *real.*"

She held out her hands toward Sam. "And you're here, and you're from Washington State. What are the odds?"

Sam waited for an explanation of this strange monologue.

"See, my dad, Lorenzo Silva, was ... um, a bit of a wanderer, my mom would say, and he worked all over the States. I know he worked near Seattle as a truck mechanic for a couple of years. He was almost always gone in the years when I was ten to twelve. I remember because my school had all these father-daughter projects, and I was mortified that my father wasn't around."

She shook her head and stared at the wall as she said, "And then later, whenever Dad *was* around and he was pissed off at me, he'd tell me he had a nicer daughter, a better daughter, in Washington State. A daughter named Maya." Turning her head, she focused again on Sam.

Sam was dumbstruck.

"Mom always said he was just teasing me."

"That's an amazing coincidence," Sam murmured.

Had Maya ever mentioned a father? Not that Sam could recall. The girl rarely even spoke about her dead, drug-addicted mother. Maya had been in so many foster homes that Sam was probably the closest thing to an adult relative she had these days.

"Maya has a little wolf carving, wonderfully detailed, like those." Sam pointed to the pronghorn and the boar on Jade's desk. "Where did you get them?"

"My dad made these." With her free hand, she caressed

the pronghorn's smooth back. "Wow again. Maya has one of my dad's carvings?"

Jade handed Sam's phone back. "So he wasn't kidding. Whoa! This is a shock. Huh. He really had another daughter?"

She shook her head, then added, "Seems like my dad kind of spread the wealth around, so to speak. I have to think about that, I guess. He was gone a lot. But he always came home, eventually. That's what counted."

Sam's emotional throttle had shot from coolly curious to blazing mad. *That's what counted? A bit of a wanderer?*

"When I met Maya," she'd told Jade, her tone frosty, "she was a foster kid working off a juvie sentence by hacking trails out of the wilderness in Olympic National Park."

The photographer took a step back, pushing her fingers through her hair. She licked her lips before saying only, "Oh." She sat back on her bed.

Sam wasn't sure the other woman got the point. "A *penniless* foster kid," she emphasized. "Her mother was a drug addict who overdosed when Maya was twelve. And I've never heard her mention a father at all."

In other words, your father never supported the child he'd fathered in Washington because Maya didn't count.

"Shit." Jade's expression had grown solemn. "I didn't know. Honestly, I didn't." After an uncomfortable moment, she'd asked, "Are there others?"

Sam snorted. "Maybe your father could answer that question."

"I'd ask if I could." Jade shrugged. "He died in 2005. Heart attack at a truck stop in Wyoming."

Sam wondered whether Lorenzo Silva had died with his pants on, but she managed to keep the nasty question from passing her lips. She'd just met Jade, and the photographer's mournful expression probably meant that she truly hadn't been aware of Maya's circumstances. Or even that Maya existed. Taking a deep breath, Sam blew the air out slowly to relax the muscles between her shoulder blades.

"Could I talk to Maya?" Jade asked hesitantly. "I know there's no guarantee, but it would be cool if we *were* half sisters, don't you think?"

"I think Maya would love to have *any* relative *anywhere*. I'll connect the two of you."

"That'd be sweet." Jade nodded her head enthusiastically.

"Jade, you'd be lucky to have Maya as a sister. She's a smart, funny, resilient young woman."

Her roommate smiled. "I look forward to meeting her."

The three of them used a Wi-Fi app to video-chat. Maya, seated at a table with her junior college coursework spread out in front of her, agreed that even though she'd never known her father's name, maybe Silva could be the man. She and Jade stared at each other so long and so intently that Sam felt like they might reach through the laptop screen to hold hands. They'd both agreed to send off DNA tests ASAP to see whether they actually were half sisters.

"ASAP" had to wait, however. Jade was in the middle of Nowhere, Arizona, and Maya had no money to invest in such an enterprise until Jade supplied the funds.

So now Jade and Maya had been emailing each other and video-chatting for nearly two weeks. Maya was considering taking up photography, or maybe videography. Maybe making nature films for television.

What happened to your plan to get an environmental science degree?, Sam had inquired about the girl's previously stated educational goal.

Maya was currently enrolled at the community college on a state subsidy for former foster kids.

Maybe I can do that afterward. Jade says you can learn a

lot about wildlife from photographing it.

Sam had gritted her teeth at the response. It was disheartening how easily she'd been supplanted by Jade as Maya's current role model.

Pulling her thoughts back to the present, Sam brought up her latest email. There was a message from Maya: Where's Jade? She's not answering her email. I want to ask her a camera question.

*Hello to you, too*, Sam thought as she typed, Jade's in the field. She'll answer when she gets back. How's college?

Sam didn't really expect a response from Maya. That was a good thing because there was none.

There was also no new message from Jade. Sam typed a quick note to her, hoping that she might receive it, wherever she was. Where are you? When will you be back? I covered for you. And finally, Can I keep the photo?

After clicking Send, Sam waited for a few minutes.

Nothing.

There were no messages from her lover, FBI Agent Chase Perez, either, nor from her housemate, Blake. Apparently, nobody missed her. Except her cat, Simon. He always missed her. A pang of guilt shot through her gut at leaving her aging feline for six weeks. But Blake was there. He'd let Simon curl up in his lap once in a while, wouldn't he?

She reminded herself that both Chase and Blake worked, and Simon didn't do email. She shouldn't really expect any news until the evening hours. Zipping a full bottle of water into her pack and grabbing her car keys, she headed for Cave Creek Canyon.

# 3

Holding her breath, Sam stayed motionless as the bird swiveled his head to fix a yellow-ringed eye on her from the sycamore branch across the trail. They studied each other for a few minutes, Sam admiring the sheen of the scarlet feathers on the trogon's breast, the shiny, ink-black cap of its hood, and the ribbon of white that separated the colors. Slowly, she inched her cell phone up. When she glanced down to select the camera function, the male trogon pivoted on his branch. With a brief flash of the green feathers on the back of his neck, he lifted his wings, displaying a glimpse of turquoise near the top of his long black tail. Elegant, indeed.

Giving a call that sounded more like a complaining squirrel than a stylish bird, the trogon flapped overhead to the tree opposite his former perch, plucked an unlucky insect from the bark, then swooped through the forest to another tree. Sam followed as quietly as she could, cell camera at the ready.

The trogon settled at the edge of a nest hole pecked into the tree trunk, probably by one of the ever-industrious flickers in the canyon. As Sam snapped photos, the gorgeous male bird stuffed a winged insect, likely a moth, into one of the screeching beaks within. Then to her delight, a female trogon landed on a nearby branch. Her coloring was less striking, with only a reddish blush to the white feathers of her lower breast and back feathers that were more army green than emerald or turquoise, but she had the same ringed eyes, heavy beak, and long, elegant tail. She, too, had brought a snack to their chicks. The squirming creature in her beak looked like a meal worm, or perhaps an unfortunate caterpillar. As soon as her mate flew away, she landed in his place and thrust the prize into an open mouth.

Sam hoped the bird parents had some way to know which chick had already been fed. It would be beyond frustrating to be the smallest baby, doomed to watch the sibling that could stretch its neck higher and open its beak wider get the majority of food.

Leaning against the smooth trunk of a cottonwood, Sam checked her photos. Several were blurs, but a few were good enough to include in the articles she'd promised to write. Her second assignment was due tomorrow, a post for Save the Wilderness Fund about the unique ecosystems here in the Sky Islands. These elegant trogons could be the stars of that article.

But she couldn't stop thinking about that jaguar. Its desperate longing tugged at her heart. How many miles would he have to roam to pass beyond that steel-and-concrete barrier? Could he still get to Mexico at all? Or was the beautiful cat a permanent prisoner on the US side?

Soft voices caught her attention. Two women were coming up the trail. As they neared, she recognized them as members of the Great Old Broads for Wilderness contingent that was currently staying at the research station. Both she and Jade had been slipping into their educational lectures—last night, a talk about a jaguar preserve in the northern state of Sonora, Mexico. Tonight, the presentation was about Mexican wolves. Checking her watch, Sam decided she'd better hustle back down the trail if she wanted to catch dinner before that program.

The women were less than fifty feet away now, approaching stealthily, their gaze roving among the tree limbs overhead, their hands clutching binoculars that dangled from straps around their necks. Birders who had received the same tip as Sam about where to find the trogons, no doubt. Catching their eyes, she held a finger to her lips and then pointed to the trogons' nest hole.

Smiling, the freckled woman mouthed a silent thank you. The other, a dark-skinned woman with close-cropped hair, used the deaf-language sign of touching fingers to her chin and then thrusting them out toward Sam.

In ninety minutes, she was back in the dorm room. Still no sign of Jade. She transferred her photos from her cell phone to her laptop and then went to find the director of the station.

The director's office was closed and locked, but Sam found the head housekeeper, Holly Tilson, restocking supplies in the laundry room. Raising her gaze from the towels she was folding, Holly asked, "What's up, Sam? You look worried."

"I am. My roommate left in the middle of the night last night. Well, early this morning, I guess, but at any rate, she hasn't been back. I know she went down by the border wall, but I don't know anything else. She was supposed to be on kitchen duty today. I had to take her shift instead."

"Your roommate is Jade Silva, right?"

"Yes."

"Ah, Jade." Holly rolled her eyes. "You know she arrived two weeks before you did."

Sam wanted to say *So?* but she settled for, "Okay."

"Twice during that time, she either showed up late for her volunteer duties or didn't show up at all."

"Oh."

Holly shook out a towel and then doubled it over. "Jade was always very apologetic, and when she showed us the incredible photos she'd taken while she was AWOL, it was hard to hold anything against her." Folding the towel again into quarters, Holly made a clucking sound with her tongue. "Still, that sort of unreliability is not fair to anyone, is it?"

Sam made a noncommittal sound in her throat.

"I know the director was considering asking her to leave before you showed up. But then for the past two weeks, you seemed to have a positive influence on her, and she showed up as promised."

"Coincidence?" Sam suggested. It was hard to believe that her mere presence could have that effect on anyone.

"Seems like it now, doesn't it? Well, bless you for taking her shift." Holly fingered the ever-present tiny gold cross that hung from a delicate chain around her neck.

"But shouldn't I . . . you . . . we be worried?" Jade was an adult, a visitor, and only a volunteer, not an employee. It was hard to know who, if anyone, should be keeping track of her.

Holly frowned. "It hasn't even been twenty-four hours yet, has it?"

"Guess not. Maybe she had car trouble or something. She hasn't called the station?" Cell phones didn't work in the mountains, but there was a functional landline in the dining hall as well as in the office.

"If she called, I haven't heard about it." Holly placed the folded towel on a stack of others and extracted a new towel from the pile on the table. "Let's wait until tomorrow morning. If Jade doesn't show up by then, I'll look up her emergency contacts and call to see whether her family has heard from her. Does she have friends in the area?"

"Damned if I know."

Holly gave her a stern look, and Sam immediately felt guilty for swearing. Or blaspheming, or whatever the transgression was. She was suddenly the preacher's daughter again, sitting beside her grandmother in a hard, wooden pew and counting her sins as her father instructed his flock from the pulpit.

Fortunately, the dinner bell rang just then, and adult Sam left before she incriminated herself further.

Before she sat down to dinner with the crowd of visiting Broads, Sam coerced Penny, one of the office staff, into giving her Jade's emergency contact information and the license plate number for Jade's red CR-V. After the meal, she used the station landline to call Jade's emergency contact, her mother, Katerina Franco. Based on the last name, Sam guessed the woman had remarried after the death of Lorenzo Silva.

The woman sounded surprised when Sam identified herself and then asked about Jade.

"Interesting," Katerina commented. "I had no idea Jade was in Arizona. But then, my daughter doesn't keep me informed about what she's up to."

Sam experienced a sudden twinge of guilt as she tried to remember the last time she'd called her father in Kansas.

"After all, she's twenty-nine years old," Katerina continued. "We don't live in each other's pockets. Jade has friends all over the country, even the world, actually, and she's always vanishing off to some remote location to get a photo of some animal she hasn't yet captured on film. Well, I guess that would be on a computer chip these days."

Katerina sounded critical, and Sam felt an urge to defend her roommate's fascination with wildlife. She wondered what her own mother, Susan Westin, would have said about Sam's habit of venturing into wild areas every chance she got. If her mother hadn't died when Sam was only nine, would they have been close?

"Summer? Sam? Are you still there?"

Katerina's words jogged her brain back to the present. She

blinked, glanced around at the empty dining hall. "Yes, sorry, I'm here. So you haven't heard from Jade lately?"

"No. Not for, oh, two months or so. Has something happened?"

"Not that I know of," Sam told her. "Jade hasn't shown up for the volunteer work she signed up for, so I'm trying to locate her."

Sam heard a sputter. "If Jade's hot on the trail of some wild animal, she wouldn't stop to do *volunteer work*." Katerina made it sound like volunteer work was akin to shoveling manure. Maybe she was emulating Jade's attitude? "Jade once dropped off the face of the earth in Zimbabwe for two solid weeks. I'd already started to organize her memorial service when she finally surfaced. She'd been camping in the bush, tracking a rare black rhino. Poachers were tracking it, too, and she was afraid to leave the rhino's side until the animal was back within a protected reserve. She even took photos of the would-be poachers."

The more Katerina told her, the more Sam found herself admiring Jade. "That took guts."

"Or a streak of insanity. She could have been killed. Thank heavens we're safe from that sort of violence in the US."

Sam wasn't so sure about that, but she decided to keep that worrisome thought to herself. "Jade's probably okay, wherever she is, but I'd still like to find her as soon as possible. And I know the staff here would, too. Can you give me the numbers of some of Jade's friends?"

"Oh, *hmmm*. Let me think . . . There's a Celia in Taos and a Susan in Albuquerque, and I think there was a Lenny or Lanny something, somewhere near the Arizona border. I don't have any numbers, unfortunately. I'm surprised I can remember the names of any of her lovers."

"Lovers?" Surprised, Sam stumbled over the word.

After a brief hesitation, Katerina said, "Jade's bi, you know."

At first, Sam heard the woman's words as "Jade's by," and she waited for the location Jade was near for a couple of seconds until she realized that Katerina was saying her daughter was bisexual.

She didn't know what Jade's sexuality had to do with anything. "Oh. I didn't know. But it doesn't make any difference to me. We're just friends."

"That's good, I guess; she doesn't seem to stay close to anyone for very long. I'll call you if I hear from her. And the next time you see her, ask her to call me once in a while, okay?"

"I will." For a few seconds, Sam debated whether to ask the woman about her philandering husband and other children he had fathered. No, this was not the time to introduce Maya into the conversation. "Thanks for speaking to me, Katerina."

After she'd hung up, Sam stared at the phone, her frustration mounting. The only other people who seemed to be concerned about Jade's absence were Maya and Bev, and both had reasons that were mostly for their own benefit, not out of worry about whether Jade Silva was in trouble.

Sam resolved to be more appreciative of her own lover, Chase Perez, and her housemate, Blake. If she failed to come home, they'd make sure her cat was fed and search for her.

And she'd call her preacher father in Kansas more often, too. Just like Jade's mother, Reverend Westin had no idea his daughter was in Arizona right now.

# 4

The lecture on Mexican gray wolves was fascinating, if a little disheartening. The population of wolves that had been reintroduced into the wild in Arizona and New Mexico was incredibly small, so to increase their genetic diversity, wildlife specialists added captive-born pups into the dens of wolves that had recently given birth. Although some packs were expanding, many wolves were still illegally killed each year, most probably by ranchers. The deaths were never investigated.

In the photos, the majority of the wild wolves wore radio collars. That sight always made Sam wince. As a wildlife biologist, she understood how valuable the data was to scientists, but the ugly, awkward collars seemed yet another human-induced cruelty.

Not being a member of the Great Old Broads organization, Sam sat near the back of the meeting room. The front row was reserved for visiting scientists, conservation group leaders, and other local dignitaries. Sam noticed a man with a ponytail sitting among them. Diego Xintal, the biologist who had lectured on jaguars the night before.

As soon as the presentation was finished, Sam slipped through the crowd and stopped Xintal as he as leaving the building. He startled when she grabbed his arm, whirling around to look at her.

"Sorry," she apologized. "Can I talk to you for a minute?"

The Broads flowed around them, chatting to one another as they passed. Sam gestured Xintal off to the side of the double exit doors.

"I'm Sam Westin." She held out her hand.

"Diego Xintal." He pronounced it "Sheen-tal."

"I heard your presentation on jaguars last night," she told him. "It was fantastic."

"Thanks." He dipped his chin and waited for more, gazing earnestly at her.

From his lecture, she knew he was Mexican by birth but was now a US citizen with an American wife. His chiseled facial structure and straight black hair, similar to Chase's, hinted at a Native American heritage. Did that term encompass Mexicans as well, or did they say "Native Mexican"? Indigenous? Indian? It was so hard to navigate the modern maze of political correctness.

*Focus*, she told herself. Dismissing all those errant thoughts, she asked, "I think you met my roommate, Jade Silva?"

"The photographer. I've known of her work for years."

"I'm guessing that she wanted to know about jaguars, and in particular, any local sightings."

"Yes." Apparently, Xintal was a man of few words.

"Did you give her any tips on where to find a jaguar?"

He hesitated, pursing his lips.

"I'm a wildlife biologist, too, so I understand that you can't share that information with just anyone, but see, Jade left our room last night, and she hasn't returned."

"Really." Raising his hand, he frowned and rubbed his jaw.

"I'm worried about her. Do you have any idea where she might be?"

"I suspect she headed down toward the border," he finally said. "I told her that a jaguar had been spotted in the Huachuca Mountains, and he seemed to be headed east."

"She found him."

His dark eyes lit up. "Amazing! Where?"

"She emailed me a photo of him at the border wall."

"The wall? Shit." Xintal tucked a strand of errant hair behind his ear. "I hope he peeled out of there before someone shot him. Way too many guns riding around down there, just waiting for an excuse to shoot something."

That was a horrible thought, that someone would kill that gorgeous cat. El Jefe's skin on eBay showed that jaguars were still desirable targets. However, it was Jade who was missing. Sam swallowed hard. "I don't know where the jaguar might have gone after that photo, and I don't know where Jade is now, either. Do you have any idea?"

Xintal folded his arms across his chest, his forehead wrinkled with concern. "Have you gone down there? To the wall?"

"Not today. I keep hoping she'll show up."

"Do you know where on the wall she took the photo?"

"No."

"Were there any signs or distinguishing features on the wall?"

"I don't think so. The photo was taken before dawn, so it's hard to tell. But it looked like heavy wire mesh with concertina wire at the top."

"Can I see that photo?"

Sam hesitated. What would Xintal tell others if he saw the photo? She didn't yet have Jade's permission to share it with anyone, and she didn't really know this man. She had no idea what sort of hornet's nest she might be poking. "I don't think I should show it to anyone without asking Jade."

He exhaled heavily. "Well, then, if you're trying to find her, I guess your best bet would be to go down there and drive along the wall and see if you find any signs of her. If the wall in her photo was wire mesh and not those tall pillars they call bollards, then it's an old section that hasn't been replaced yet, probably somewhere between Douglas and Naco. I'd head to the wall a few miles short of Naco and start driving east along the wall. Or start near Douglas and drive west."

Xintal paused, stared intently into her eyes for a long moment. "And don't let the border patrol give you any shit. We are all Americans. We have a right to drive on American roads and see that damn wall we're paying for, whenever we damn well please."

His scowl told Sam that Diego Xintal had been hassled many times by the authorities. "If Jade doesn't show up during the night, I'll go down there tomorrow," she told him. "Thanks."

"Good luck. Be careful." With a final nod, Xintal walked off into the dark.

Pulling a penlight from her pocket, she walked back to the dorm, checking the path ahead for snakes. The evening was already growing cold, but she didn't want to trip over a rattlesnake, even if it would be slowed down by the dropping temperature.

Her dorm room was still empty. Sam opened her window to let in the evening sounds and then plopped down in her desk chair to check email on her laptop.

I miss you was the subject line of a message from Chase. She opened it to discover that he was working a case on the Makah reservation, way out on the westernmost tip of Washington State. After Special Agent Starchaser Perez had switched from the FBI office in Salt Lake City to a job in Washington State, Sam had hoped that her lover would be around more often. He had purchased an old cabin less than twenty miles from her, and they were working together on remodeling it. But now he was a solo act, working with the many Native American tribes spread across the Northwest, so these days he was still away from home more often than not.

I'm in a rustic cabin with a view of the ocean, he reported. Wish you were here.

I'm in a dorm room with a view of the Chiricahua peaks, she replied. I wish you were here. Cool place. I'm learning a lot, but I miss my cat.

She clicked Send and then waited a beat.

A new message appeared on the screen. Your *cat?*

The internet connection was fast tonight. Grinning, she typed, Of course I miss Simon! And Blake. And—oh yeah—this hunky FBI agent I love to kiss.

Which FBI agent would that be?

*Te quiero,* Chase. She didn't understand why it was always easier for her to say "I love you" in Spanish, but it was. And *buenos noches.*

*Buenas noches,* he corrected. *Yo te amo más, querida.*

She'd been with him long enough to understand "I love you even more, sweetheart."

Impossible, she typed. But I need to go to bed now.

Me too. Be careful. Stay out of trouble. Good night.

*Stay out of trouble?* She was certainly going to try. But it seemed like trouble had found her, or at least, her roommate. After pulling up Photoshop, she opened the jaguar picture. Was there anything that could identify the location of that photo? There was no convenient GPS marker or town name. The corner of some sort of label could be seen on the metal mesh of the fence, just above and to the right of the jaguar's outstretched paw. Looked like a strip of metal engraved with letters. Maybe a *T* followed by an *H*? It was hard to make out.

But she made a mental note of it. Maybe it could help locate the photo.

Through the fence, on the Mexican side, she could see the upright arms of a tall saguaro in the distance, standing like a cross on a hill. That cactus could be a landmark for someone who knew the area. She zoomed in on the vegetation there to see whether she could sharpen it more, then gasped and sat back in her chair. Were those *eyes*? Leaning forward, she zoomed in more. The image was pixelated now instead of smooth, but the patterns of those little squares were unmistakable.

"Oh my God," she murmured aloud.

Its outline was obscured by brush, and its spotted fur was nearly indistinguishable from the leaves that surrounded it, but as she fiddled with contrast and colors, she was sure she was looking at a second jaguar.

A potential mate?

The two jaguars that had been seen in Arizona in recent years were both males, probably young cats searching for their own territories. Now one was dead, killed for its beautiful skin. But across the border, at least a dozen jaguars, both male and female, lived in a reserve in the mountains of northern Mexico.

On the other side of that blasted wall.

She looked up Naco to make sure where the town was located. According to Wikipedia, Naco was very small, only a little more than a wide spot in the road, with the ruins of old adobe buildings that were once Fort Naco, a military outpost established in the early twentieth century. A larger town on the Mexican side of the border was also named Naco, which seemed to imply a distinct lack of imagination on the part of one or both nations. Or maybe it had originally been one town and was now divided by the border.

Apparently, Naco, Arizona held the questionable honor of

being the only place in the continental US to be bombed by a foreign power, or actually by a mercenary operating for a foreign power. That incident had taken place in 1929 during an uprising in Mexico when a pilot had accidentally dropped his load on the Arizona side of the border.

Sam shook her head. Border walls and accidental bombings. Humans had always been an especially vindictive species.

YouTube played a video documenting how the American residents of Naco, including many children, had painted friendly murals on their side of the fence. Then the US Army had replaced the painted section with a bollard wall sporting miles of concertina wire looping from top to bottom. Any child attempting to paint there again would be shredded.

Sam groaned. How depressing.

An owl hooted somewhere in the forest that bordered the research station.

She had no volunteer duties tomorrow. Sam knew where she was headed at first light.

Her email notice dinged, and she switched back to her in-box. A new message from Maya: Jade isn't answering me. Anything wrong?

Sam debated between "I hope not" and an outright lie, then she finally chickened out entirely, deciding it was best not to answer. She changed into her sleepwear and turned out the light, hoping she would be able to reassure Maya tomorrow morning.

When she closed her eyes, all she could see was that jaguar stretching his full length against that barrier of metal mesh and razor-sharp wire.

The lush vegetation and the second cat on the other side.

The intensity of the jaguar's longing had burned the image into her brain.

Another owl hooted somewhere close to her open window. A great horned, she thought. Then there was an answer from the first owl. Maybe a male and female, conversing in the darkness.

Sleep was a long time coming.

# 5

Sam could no longer stand to look at Jade's rumpled covers, so just after dawn, she made both beds, tucking the sheets and blankets tight around the thin mattresses. She didn't want to wait for breakfast in the dining hall, so she smeared a couple of crackers with the peanut butter she kept on her shelf and called it good.

The drive from the nearby settlement of Portal to Douglas took her more than an hour. Between Douglas and Naco, Diego Xintal had suggested. Soon she could see the border wall in the distance, and a few miles west of Douglas, she turned onto a gravel access road and headed for the barrier. As far as she could see, the landscape was gray, brushy country. So dry and dusty it made her throat itch just to view it. If a fire ever got started here, it would pour over these hills like a flash flood. That image made her think about all the animals that would need to run from a fire. And what they'd encounter if they ran south. She shook her head, trying to erase the mental picture of barbecued wildlife and ranchers' cattle all along the border fence, and nearly swerved into the ditch.

*Get a grip, Westin*, she reprimanded herself, easing her foot off the accelerator and watching the road more carefully. A roadrunner raced her for a few yards, and tumbleweeds puffed jerkily along the route, propelled by the gusty winds.

She passed a low cement building and a fenced lot full of green-striped border patrol SUVs, and wondered whether they'd soon be tailing her.

At the wall, she parked her car in the gravel and got out to take photographs. No other vehicle was in view. The rolling hills were divided by arroyos, now just dry washes. For as far as she could see, the metal border wall marched up and down the landscape like the rust-colored fin of some giant, belligerent dinosaur.

The fence was whining and growling like a demonic beast, too, the wind playing a nerve-grating tune on the metal structures. How did the locals stand that noise?

The wall in front of her did not match the structure in Jade's photo. Returning to her RAV4, Sam turned west and drove slowly along it, amazed by the patchwork of panels. Some were mesh, some were layers of horizontal rails fastened to posts, others were upright and solid. All of them appeared to be scalable by any determined human, but not by any animal that didn't possess wings.

A white SUV with a distinctive green stripe barreled down the border road toward her. As it passed, the green-uniformed border patrol agent inside twisted his head and gave her a hard look. She waved, and he then focused on the road ahead and zoomed off in a cloud of dust.

So far, so good. Probably helped to be a small blond woman.

She crawled along in low gear, inspecting the wall and the surrounding countryside as she went, searching for any sign of Jade or her red CR-V. Tumbleweeds had piled up against the Mexican side of the wall, and in the low washes, the brushy spheres were also joined by branches and trash obviously swept there by a stream. Clearly, the barrier had not been designed to allow for the rapid flow of water after a deluge. She knew the wall had caused flooding on both sides of the border, and Mexicans had actually drowned because of debris dams on their side. She idly wondered how long it would take for a pile to rise high enough on the upstream side that a border crosser could simply scale the heap of driftwood and garbage and jump over the wall? That might be the salvation for wildlife needing to cross. But she saw no ramps of flotsam on the Arizona side—only on the Sonoran side.

In one dry wash, she spied a torn red daypack among the debris, as well as several wads of clothing; in another, a single, faded, child-size tennis shoe. She wondered what their stories were. Desperate families, drug smugglers, or just detritus dropped by the Sonoran ranchers whose property bordered the wall? No people were visible on the Mexican side; the landscape south of the wall was eerily vacant.

The terrain on the US side was nearly as empty and far more barren. No red CR-V. In nearly twenty miles, only two more border patrol vehicles passed her, one traveling each direction along the road that paralleled the wall. She spotted three more parked on narrow side roads that gutted the arid landscape. A couple of hilltop towers watched silently. She suspected they were surveillance stations.

Lonely.

Creepy.

She felt as if she'd traveled back in time and was driving through a hostile foreign country, like she imagined divided Berlin had looked and felt. Adding to the military atmosphere, occasional clusters of vehicles with camouflage paint were grouped along the wall, and men in fatigues, some with clipboards in hand, walked along its base. US Army Corps of Engineers, she supposed. She'd heard that a lot of them had been deployed to the border.

She got so lost in counting all the access roads and trying

to spot patrol vehicles in the brush that she had to suddenly brake to a stop when she realized she was passing a wall section that seemed familiar. Her wheels kicked up a cloud of dust that blew northward.

Pulling out her cell phone, she brought up the altered photo she'd copied there. After taking a swig of water from her bottle, she pulled on a baseball cap against the harsh sun and slid out of her RAV4.

The mesh panel in front of her matched the mesh under the jaguar's paws in the photo, but this panel had a horizontal bar that the photograph didn't contain. She walked down the line, comparing the photo with the fence panels. A gust of wind puffed dust into her face. The fence whined like a creature that was suffering.

*There.* A crossbar high above her head on the right side of the mesh panel read THORENSEN, the name looking as if it had been cut into the metal with a blowtorch. Hooking her fingers through the heavy rust-colored mesh, she surveyed the greenery on the Mexican side. No jaguar was visible in the shrubs there, but she recognized the lone saguaro standing tall on the highest hill.

This was it, the location of Jade's photo.

A slight whining noise overhead caught Sam's attention, and when she studied the sky to find its source, she saw a quick glint of sun off a metallic surface. A drone, no doubt. Probably belonged to border patrol.

After checking the ground at her feet, Sam strolled across the road, studying the dirt. Not a single paw print or even a human footprint, other than those made by her own small hiking boots. She saw only tire impressions and what might be sweep or drag marks, as if the road had been scoured free of prints of all kinds.

What the heck? Only a bit more than twenty-four hours

had passed. It hadn't rained. Could the gusty breeze erase all marks in that short amount of time? She doubted it.

Raising a hand to her brow, she scanned the area to the north for any sign of Jade's SUV. No hint of red anywhere, but a dust cloud was headed directly for her on an access road that cut through the hills. As it neared, she was amazed to see a food truck, a large blue van with a TACO LOBO sign on its side.

A taco truck, out here in the middle of nowhere? That seemed improbable. It was headed west, so it had probably come from Douglas. Maybe this was its regular route. She wanted to talk to the driver. She waved an arm in his direction, but he didn't acknowledge her, so she stepped into the road and raised both arms over her head.

The taco truck skidded to a stop in the gravel, sending a cloud of dust her way. The driver's window rolled down, and a darkly tanned, middle-aged man leaned his head out. "What the hell, lady? You lookin' to get killed?"

"I want to ask you a question." Sam pulled her cell phone out of her pocket.

"I can't give you a ride."

"That's not it." She held up her phone with Jade's photo on the screen. "I'm looking for this woman. She was driving a red Honda CR-V, and she was right here yesterday morning."

"So? I wasn't here then. Now get out of my way."

Sam gazed at the rear of the truck, wondering whether he had helpers riding in the kitchen area. "Are you alone? Maybe—"

"None of your fucking business!" The window rolled up as he floored the accelerator. The wheels spun in the gravel, then finally found traction, and the taco truck zoomed off, the dust cloud rolling behind it.

*What the hell?* Choking on a breath of dust, Sam watched the Taco Lobo truck speed down the road. The border patrol should definitely stop that guy. Who knew what he was hauling in the back?

Maybe the patrol was tracking the taco truck, because now she saw another vehicle approaching at high speed, a white SUV with a diagonal green stripe.

Unlike the others that had driven past earlier, this border patrol vehicle rocked to a stop in the road beside her. As she held her hand over her mouth, coughing at the dust it kicked up, the driver's window rolled down.

A heavy-set man with a blond buzz cut leaned out. "Let's see some ID."

She coughed again, waving a hand in front of her face, then swallowed before she spoke. "What? Did you see that taco truck peel out of here?"

"I saw it. Identification," he barked. "Proof of citizenship."

"What?" she said again. "Why are you asking me for that?"

His partner, an olive-skinned man with dark hair and mirrored sunglasses, slid out of the passenger seat and walked around to stand in front of her, his arms crossed against his chest. The name tag on his green uniform identified him as J. Alvarez. "We don't need a reason, ma'am," he explained. "What did you just put in your pocket?"

She tapped her pants pocket. "A cell phone."

Buzz Cut slid from the passenger seat and held out a hand, palm up, in her direction. "Let's see it. Now." R. Bradley, according to his right chest pocket. When she hesitated, Bradley let his hand drop to the pistol he wore on his hip.

She recalled Xintal's advice from last night. *Don't let them give you any shit.*

*Yeah, right.* Pulling out her cell phone, she handed it over.

Bradley thumbed it back to life and both border patrol agents studied the photo of the jaguar.

"Whoa!" Alvarez remarked. "Really?"

"Interesting," Bradley concluded. "Did you take this?"

"No. I got it from a friend. I was trying to find the spot where she took it."

He swiped across the screen a few times to display other photos Sam had taken.

"Hey!" she complained. "Don't mess with those. I don't think you're supposed to be doing that."

Bradley snorted. After swiping and viewing a few more photos, he handed the phone back to her. "Let's see that ID now."

"I have a driver's license in my car." She slid the phone back into her pocket and pointed at her RAV4, a hundred yards down the road.

"Let's get it." He strode off toward her SUV.

Sam tried to match his stride, hustling along by his side. Alvarez followed, his footsteps heavy behind her. When she glanced back at him, she noticed that he, too, had his hand on his pistol.

When they reached her RAV4, she put her hand on the door handle, but Bradley clasped her arm, pulled her away, and opened the door himself.

She rubbed her arm. "My wallet's in the glove compartment."

Bradley retrieved her wallet, then glanced at his partner and tilted his head toward the rear of her SUV. Alvarez pulled open the back door and began rifling through the cargo area.

"Hey!" she said again. "What gives you the right to do that?"

Bradley studied her driver's license. "Washington State. You're a long way from home." He glanced up, and she saw her own face mirrored in his sunglasses. "A driver's license is not proof of citizenship."

"It's all I have with me. I am in my own country, after all."

"What are you *really* doing here?" Bradley handed her wallet back to her.

"Like I said, trying to find the spot where that photo was taken. And looking for the photographer."

"Oh yeah?"

"Yeah," she snapped as she pulled out her phone again and swiped through the photos for one of Jade.

Alvarez shut the back door of her RAV4 and reappeared beside them. "Daypack. Water, snacks, spare tire and jack, extra oil," he reported to Bradley. "And clothes—all her size."

Grimacing at the intrusion, Sam located a photo of Jade sitting on her bed in the dorm room, legs crossed in lotus position, a bowl of popcorn in her lap. She held it out to the agents. "This is the photographer, Jade Silva. Have you seen her?"

The two men took their time studying the image.

"Pretty," Alvarez commented.

"Have you seen her? She would have been right here a little more than twenty-four hours ago."

"Hard to say. Ninety percent of the girls that come through here look like that." Bradley handed the phone back. "Which side of the border did she come from?"

"This side." Gritting her teeth, Sam pointed to the ground at her feet. "Jade Silva is an American."

"That right?"

"Yes. She was driving a dark-red Honda CR-V, this year's model. Have you seen her car?"

Both agents simply stared at her.

"You'd have video of cars driving along this road, wouldn't you?"

"Yep," Alvarez acknowledged.

"Like that taco truck, for example. The driver had an attitude; he seemed suspicious to me. He could be carrying anything in the back."

"Most likely tacos. Workers gotta eat out here." Bradley turned back toward the patrol vehicle. "Move along, Miz Westin."

"Wait!" Sam yelped. "Can you look for Jade's car? Or can I see the video?"

Bradley ignored her and walked down the road.

Before he followed his partner, Alvarez told her, "Have a nice day."

Sam had heard that Mexican kids sometimes chucked rocks at border patrol agents. Now she understood why.

# 6

As soon as the agents had driven away, Sam returned to her search of the ground, following her own footprints down and across the road, moving back and east until she could match the angle of the photo. The position next to a rugged access road appeared to be the approximate location Jade would have stood in. The dirt at Sam's feet held the same strange smooth marks, as if someone had used a broom on the ground. Weird.

She backtracked down the road and finally came across tire tracks that could have belonged to Jade's SUV. Or to a dozen other vehicles. No boot prints. Moving off the graded road into the brushy desert beyond, she began scrutinizing the ground again, zigzagging among the thorny shrubs, searching for prints. In a bush, she found a plastic cap from a fast-food soda cup, still impaled by a plastic straw.

Not helpful. And it didn't seem like an item that would have been dropped by a migrant traveling through the desert, either. Pushing it into her pocket, she continued zigzagging toward a group of large tan-colored boulders, expecting more border patrol agents to arrive at any moment.

The ground between the shrubs was patterned with shoe prints leading in every direction. Shredded clothing was caught here and there in the thorny brush. No item was intact; each had rips and pieces missing. One shoe lurked in the shadow of a boulder. Under another large rock were two water bottles, flattened and punctured by something sharp. A woman's bra, stained and with a torn strap, hung from a cactus. The area looked as if it had been the site of repeated altercations among the migrants passing through, as if they'd torn one another apart. But why?

All the human debris seemed a desecration to the natural landscape. The land in this area belonged mostly to the US Forest Service. Whose job was it to clean this up? The forest service rangers? The border patrol? Trying to ignore all the distracting detritus, Sam searched the ground for animal tracks. Unless it had followed the wall for miles, odds were good that the jaguar had to walk back through this area toward the mountains. And Jade might have followed him.

She checked her phone. Two bars. She called the closest office of forest service in the Coronado National Forest and described the situation to the ranger who answered.

"A jaguar? I wish," he said. "I'd love to see one. As for your friend, I'll put the word out about her and her CR-V, but as you probably know, there could be a lot of hikers passing through all our areas, especially at night. Most try to avoid the few rangers we've got on staff."

Sam gave him her contact information, thanked him, and ended the call, frustrated. She continued her ground search.

Just as she was about to give up, in a spot of powdery dust she found a paw print. Four distinctive toes, no claws. Triangular pad. A big feline. Judging by the size, the print had been left by either a large cougar or the jaguar. She was betting on the latter. The cat was headed away from the wall, angling back toward the mountains, but this time, toward the Sky Island area she'd come from. The Pendregosa mountains, according to the label on her printed map. She'd only heard them called the Chiricahuas, with Chiricahua National

Monument at the northern tip. The mountains she called home, the Cascades and the Olympics, were long chains of high peaks. Here the mountains poked up in clusters, and every cluster of peaks had a different name.

She followed faint marks in the gravelly dirt, then spotted another paw print in the dust. Then she finally found a print left by a hiking boot. A small one, only a little larger than her own. That could be Jade's. She took a photo of it, then hiked on, trying to find more. The sun felt harsh on her skin, even at this early hour.

The prints headed back toward the access road. Then, between thorn bushes that formed an unfriendly half-circle, she found a mishmash of partial shoeprints. One looked like the toe of a treaded hiking boot, another like the heel of a cowboy boot. Drag marks, as if someone had tried to obscure them or had towed something heavy across them. And in the middle of all the prints was a huge splotch of dark, reddish-brown sand.

Sam's heartbeat quickened at the sight. Blood? Squatting, she pressed a fingertip to the red stain.

Did that sand feel slightly damp? She examined her finger. No, the dirt was dry.

*Way too many guns riding around down there, just waiting for an excuse to shoot at something.*

Could it be the jaguar's blood? Jade's? Some unlucky migrant? Feeling more nauseous with every guess, Sam stood up again and studied her surroundings. She couldn't see a surveillance tower from here, so unless one of the patrol's drones happened to be flying overhead, whatever had happened here had probably occurred out of view of the border patrol. She took several photos in all directions.

She dug her fingers into her pants pockets. Car key. A tube of lip gloss. One unused facial tissue. The tissue would have to suffice. After smoothing it out flat on the sandy ground, Sam used her car key to lift a tiny portion of the red-brown soil and position it on the tissue, which she then folded and rolled until the final package was about the size of her lip gloss.

Her cell phone now indicated no coverage. How to mark the spot? A large boulder loomed only a short distance away. She walked to it, then used a smaller rock to scratch a big X into its side. It occurred to her that the border patrol might believe she was marking a drug drop or a safe route for migrants. At this point, she didn't care.

She followed the drag marks to the access road, where they vanished into the gravel. She crisscrossed the road a number of times, checking for more prints on either side, but located nothing of interest except for a horned lizard hunkered down in a patch of shade. Either the owners of those shoeprints had driven away or walked out on the road, leaving no prints in the sharp gravel there.

The sun was almost directly overhead now, and the wind felt like a blow dryer desiccating her entire body. How did people live in this oven? She needed to hunker down in her own patch of shade, or at least go back to her car and her water bottle. But she was reluctant to leave without finding more clues.

Scrambling to the top of the nearest boulder, she studied her surroundings. A low gray-beige house was nestled into a hill less than a half mile away, nearly blending into the arid landscape. The roof was covered with solar panels. The structure was probably mostly underground for climate control if the builder had been smart and local.

Turning in place, she scanned the entire area. In the far distance, a utility van was nestled between a boulder and a spindly tree. The van was the color of dirt, sort of a dull gray brown, or maybe that was simply because it was coated in dust.

The dark windows made it impossible to discern whether there was anyone inside; it might have been abandoned. She saw no sign of a red CR-V, a spotted cat, or—God forbid—a woman's body lying in the brush.

A border patrol vehicle drove by on the access road. The green-and-white SUV abruptly halted, then she saw a flash of binocular lenses as the driver scrutinized her. She waved in his direction. After a few seconds, he waved back and drove away toward the border wall.

She climbed down from the boulder and walked back to her RAV4, estimating the distance to be a little more than a half mile. Some helpful border patrol agent had left a bright-pink notice on the windshield, warning that the car would be towed if not removed by 5:00 p.m.

The interior of her SUV was an oven and the steering wheel a branding iron, and for a distance she had to drive using only her fingertips with all the windows down before she had any sense that the air conditioner was working at all. The water in her bottle tasted like stewed plastic, but at least it was wet.

After driving the border road toward the access road she'd crossed while walking, she turned north on it and crawled slowly along, still scanning for clues. *Damn it, Jade, where are you?*

A dust-covered, dented mailbox with the name STRAUB on it marked an intersection where a rough track took off to the east. Sam followed it and soon found herself at that low house she'd spotted earlier. She parked in a space surrounded by a low dust-covered fence, then walked to the front door along a gritty sidewalk.

The structure was indeed built into the side of a hill, and the architecture was intriguing. The bottoms of glass bottles dotted the thick concrete around the darkened front windows, and the wooden front door had a hexagonal arch and a round glass window, through which she could see a short, tiled entryway with another matching door at the far end. When she pressed the doorbell, she heard a distant chime.

A darkly tanned, white-haired, mustachioed man peered intently at her through the window at the other end of the hall, then jerked the door open and strode her way. His eyeglasses were Coke-bottle thick, enlarging his watery hazel eyes to an unnatural size. He wore charcoal-colored shorts and a blue short-sleeved shirt, buttoned only halfway up his gray-haired chest. When he opened the door, she noticed his feet were bare against the terra-cotta tile floor.

He didn't appear happy to see her. "What?" he demanded, looking her up and down.

"Hi, I'm Summer Westin," she said, using her birth name. She thrust out a hand.

He ignored it. "So? What do you want?"

"I'm sorry to interrupt your day, but I'm trying to find a friend, a woman, who disappeared close to here, and I wondered whether you'd seen anything."

"Huh. I see a lot." He ran his index finger and thumb over his mustache. "Was she a UDA?"

"Pardon?"

"Undocumented alien," he translated. "U-D-A. That's what border patrol calls 'em." He snorted. "Well, that's the nicest thing the patrol calls 'em."

"She's American." Sam pulled out her phone, thumbed it to life, then showed him Jade's photo. "Her name's Jade Silva, and she's from Santa Fe. She was driving a new red CR-V. She was down near the wall before dawn yesterday-"

"Before dawn? What the hell was she doing there in the middle of the night?"

A rumble started up behind them, and Sam glanced back

over her shoulder. A convoy of huge army vehicles was grinding past on the access road, throwing up a cloud of dust that billowed toward the house.

"Crapola." The man grabbed her arm and dragged her inside, then quickly shut the door behind her. "Hate them goddamn army guys and all their goddamn construction trucks. They wake us up at 4:00 a.m. driving down to the goddamn wall and then they bury us in dust driving back at noon."

The door at the end of the hallway opened. A petite silver-haired woman stood there. "Carl!" she barked.

He swiveled to face her. "It's true, ain't it, Frannie? Half the locals are in on it, too, lining their pockets." Turning back to Sam, he added, "And then, all the live-long day *and* night, the damn patrol hot-rods around everywhere, including *our* property."

He pointed out the front window. Through the blowing dust, a swath of destruction cut across the landscape. Tire tracks slashed through a fallen cactus, and a yucca had been flattened to the ground.

"I take it you're not a fan of the border patrol?" Sam murmured softly.

"Huh," Carl snorted.

"My husband doesn't like anyone," his wife told her. "I'm Frannie Straub. Come in, dear." She gestured toward the interior of the house.

"At least the wetbacks are quiet," he grumbled, trailing behind. "Although they're more *dust*backs here." He laughed at his own joke.

"Enough," Frannie said.

Sam introduced herself to the woman and explained again that she was looking for Jade and her CR-V.

The house was amazingly cool and spacious inside, with

stucco walls and tiled floors enclosed within more poured-concrete walls dotted with embedded bottles arranged in artistic patterns. They stood in the living area, which flowed into a dining area and an open kitchen. She admired several paintings on the wall, swirls of color flowing together. "Those are nice. The one with the stripe reminds me of a waterfall."

"I can't paint anything realistic," Frannie explained. "So I do abstracts instead."

From a dog bed near the wall, a golden cocker spaniel regarded Sam with curious eyes. On the top of the dining table was a bowl of oranges and lemons, and, alarmingly, a rifle, along with a rod and cleaning supplies.

Sam immediately thought of the blood she'd found. "Are you hunters?"

"Not really," Frannie answered. "But Carl does like to shoot once in a while."

"Need a gun around here," Carl grunted as he sat down behind the table. "You gonna whack a rattlesnake with a frying pan?"

"Have you ever seen a big cat here, like a cougar or a jaguar?" Sam asked.

"Nope." Carl shook his head. "But the lions are out there. And if one comes calling, it's gonna be sorry. Don't think there are any jaguars left in Arizona, are there? So far, I've only shot coyotes. Have to protect my Goldie."

At that, the spaniel stood and walked over to Carl, placing her head beneath his outstretched hand. After patting her, Carl grasped the box of cleaning cloths and extracted one. "Sometimes I use the rifle to scare off one of them dustbacks what's wandering around the yard in the dark."

Sam gulped. What if Jade had been following the jaguar in the dark?

"He fires over their heads," Frannie informed her.

Carl shot his wife an annoyed look. "Not always."

Could Carl see well enough with those Coke-bottle glasses to distinguish what he was aiming at? "Shot anything recently?" Sam asked. *Or anyone?*

"Not since I got that fella." He tilted his head at a large rattlesnake skin on the wall.

Sam's mind remained on the gun. "Do you often hear gunshots in this area?"

"All the effin' time," Carl said.

"Lately? Like yesterday morning?"

Frannie asked her husband, "Was that yesterday, Carl? Those shots we heard?"

He shrugged. "Dunno. I remember hearing shots, but was it yesterday or the day before?"

"At least three," Frannie added. "Bam, bam. Then there was another, or maybe even one more later."

"Probably ranchers shooting at coyotes. The animal kind," Carl clarified. "Or maybe drug runners shooting at each other. Or the patrol shooting at drug runners. Sooner or later, a bullet'll come through one of these walls."

"Back to your concerns, dear." Frannie faced Sam again. "We haven't seen your friend or her car, I'm afraid. There's always something going on down at the wall, but we try to mind our own business."

"However," Carl added, "once in a while, I fire off a round or two, just to remind the goddamn patrol that I have rights and I have guns."

"I understand," Sam said, even though she didn't have a clue what good more guns would do. She studied the interior of the house. "This is a beautiful home. It's so cool inside."

"They call it an Earthship design," Frannie told her. Crossing her arms over her chest, the older woman sighed heavily. "This was our dream house. We're completely self-sufficient. We used to have a fantastic garden . . ."

"Before the aliens picked it clean and the patrol hot-rodded over it," her husband growled.

"We had a gorgeous view of the Sonoran hills." Frannie pointed to the south, where the border wall loomed, a huge rusty hulk that slashed the horizon in two.

Another deep rumble vibrated through the tile floor, and a wave of dust rolled past the front window.

"Now, we're living in a goddamn war zone," Carl growled. "Border patrol, army engineers, and everyone else they hire. They start before dawn. Sometimes they don't finish before sunset." His magnified hazel eyes fixed on her through his thick lenses. "Want to buy a house?"

Sam forced a chuckle, even though she understood the situation was far from humorous. She took a step toward the entry. "I better be going."

Frannie walked her to the door. "I hope you find your friend, dear." A basket of what looked like pieces of old T-shirts was positioned to the side of the exit. Frannie plucked a blue rag from the basket and handed it to Sam. "Take this. We have plenty."

Sam stared in confusion at the piece of cloth in her hands.

"You'll see. Goodbye."

When she found her RAV4 covered in an inch of dust, Sam snorted. She was grateful for the rag to clean off the windshield and side mirrors so she could see to return down the long driveway.

Just as she reached the road, a trio of white trucks drove past: a flatbed with several of the old mesh helicopter landing pads and coils of concertina wire strapped onto its back section, and two monster pickups loaded with generators and construction gear. On the side of one of the trucks was a logo, a circle encompassing the letters *RTK*. Obviously private companies, not army vehicles. Then her view of the trucks, the road, and everything else was obliterated by the cloud of dust blasting from beneath their tires and rolling across her windshield. Sam quickly punched the button that prevented her air conditioner from sucking in outside air.

A sharp spasm of longing for her Pacific Northwest home washed over her. She craved the view of greenery surrounding her home in the woods. She wanted to breathe cool, moist air blowing in off the Salish Sea.

The poor Straubs.

# 7

It was nearly 1:00 p.m., and Sam hadn't brought lunch, so she retraced her route and headed for Bisbee, a funky, small hill town that appealed to her sense of whimsy. Bisbee had historically been a large frontier settlement centered around a mine that produced gold, copper, silver, lead, and zinc. In the old town center, the buildings appeared to have sprung from the local rock landscape like an exotic species of fungus. Painted in a variety of bright colors, many of the houses, hotels, and apartments perched precariously on the cliffs, snuggled beneath overhangs, and wrapped around rock protrusions.

There didn't seem to be many right angles in the structures. Steep staircases were everywhere. Some buildings were so lopsided that Sam wondered whether they were safe, but most seemed to be still in use. The mine had closed way back in the seventies and was now used as the centerpiece for a local museum. Art galleries and antique shops had taken over many of the old buildings.

A tiny café advertised all-natural ingredients and had a sign in the window that broadcast the message HUMANITARIAN AID IS NOT A CRIME. Sam sat in its tiny courtyard, which was shaded by a cliff and bordered by shrubbery, a miniature oasis in the arid region. She ordered iced tea, a cup of vegetable soup, and a portobello sandwich. While she often ate meat, she loved good vegetarian cooking when she could find it.

"What can you tell me about the sign in your window?" she asked the aproned young woman who took her order.

"Just what it says." The woman hesitated and then arched an eyebrow. "You're not from around here, are you?"

Sam shook her head. "Washington State."

"Then you might not know that decent Americans giving food or water to border crossers here are not only getting arrested, they're getting convicted and sentenced."

Sam frowned. So now if someone begged her for a drink of water, she needed to demand to see a passport before she could hand over a glassful? "I'm sorry to hear that," she murmured.

"Aren't we all." The server's eyes glittered, and her mouth twisted as if she wanted to say more. But instead, she walked away, returning to the kitchen.

What could she do next to search for Jade? Despite Diego's Xintal's advice, surely it was counterproductive to simply drive all the backroads and hope to catch a glimpse of her roommate or her CR-V. Based on their ubiquitous presence along the wall, the border patrol seemed likely to have video or some sort of other information about Jade. How could she get them to share it with her?

She called Chase. She knew he was likely to be working, but as a solo FBI agent, his hours were not regular. He could be doing anything right now.

A gray tabby strolled out of the bushes next to her table and rubbed against her calves. As she waited for Chase to answer, she reached down to pet the cat's soft fur, wishing it were her own Simon. It was understandable why pets were not allowed at the Southwestern Research Station, but six weeks was a long time to spend without a cat.

"*Querida*," Chase breathed sexily into the phone.

Sam was poised to answer in the same tone when she heard a female voice in the background croon in a sing-song tone, "Oh, Romeo, Romeo!"

Sam straightened in her chair. Its metal legs grated on the flagstone beneath. "Is that Nicole?" she asked, naming Chase's former FBI partner from Salt Lake.

The tabby leaped uninvited into her lap, turning its hind end toward her, showing her that he was a neutered male, like her Simon.

"That's how you greet me?" Chase's voice returned to normal. "Ignore her."

"What's Nicole doing there?" When Sam had met Chase Perez, he had been partnered with Special Agent Nicole Boudreaux. Nicole was always immaculate, competent, and quick-witted, no matter how filthy and perplexing the situation. Around her, Sam felt disheveled, inept, and inarticulate.

The cat swished his fluffy tail across her face, adding to her current sense of awkwardness.

"This case involves a casino company out of Nevada," Chase told Sam, "so Nicole's here to provide coordination on that end. We're enjoying a reunion."

"I'll bet." Grabbing the cat's tail, Sam pushed the tabby's hind end down into a sitting position. She wasn't sure that she wanted Chase to *enjoy* working with his old partner. But she respected Nicole, even liked her, so . . .

Chase cut into her thoughts. "What's going on in the wilds of Arizona, Summer?"

The cat pivoted to face her, fixing her with his green-eyed gaze.

"Do you by any chance have any pull with the border patrol?" she asked.

"Why?"

She told Chase about Jade going missing. "The border wall between Naco and Douglas is the last place where I know she was. She might have stopped and given food or water to someone."

He didn't respond for a long moment, and she knew he was trying to sort out the logic of her last statement. She added, "Did you know that people are getting arrested down here for helping undocumented migrants?"

"Yes, I've heard that."

Sometimes, as a federal law enforcement officer, Chase's attitudes, at least the ones he expressed, were annoyingly vague. His heritage was half Lakota and half Mexican. He'd told her once that nobody knew whether his grandfather Perez had been a legal immigrant. Chase had to be conflicted about the immigration issue, didn't he?

But she knew he'd never say anything critical about a federal policy out loud, especially over the airwaves. The FBI motto was Fidelity, Bravery, Integrity. Sometimes she thought Chase took the fidelity pledge a little too far. No government agency, in fact no agency of any kind, could be perfect.

*Let it go*, she told herself, scratching the cat under its chin. "Seems like the border patrol would have video of Jade. Wouldn't they?"

"You want the border patrol to share their surveillance videos with you?"

Nicole made a scoffing noise in the background, then said, "Not going to happen."

"Please put me on speaker so you can both hear, Chase." Sam waited until he did that, then said, "I'm not joking here, you two."

The cat abruptly decided that he wanted to use her cell phone and hooked his paw around her wrist, claws out. "Ow," she yelped. "Stop that!"

"What?"

"Not you, Chase."

The server came into the courtyard, carrying Sam's order. She took one glance at the cat and hissed "Freddie, down!" The cat took off, back into the bushes. *Sorry*, the server mouthed.

"What's going on?" Chase asked.

"Just a little feline interaction." Sam wondered what Simon was up to at the moment.

"I should have known."

"Anyhow, back to my dilemma. Like I said, my roommate, another volunteer, Jade Silva, is missing, and I need some hint, any hint, of where to look. She was last seen taking a photo by the wall. I've located the exact spot she took the photo, but there's no sign of her or her car. I called the Forest Service. They haven't seen her. Anything could have happened, right? She vanished more than thirty hours ago. She could be injured, she could have been kidnapped or killed by drug smugglers, she could have been arrested by the border patrol. Where am I supposed to start? Where would *you* start?"

"Have you tried the local sheriff?" Nicole asked.

*Damn.* Why hadn't she thought of that? "I will. But what if he—or she—has no information?"

"Nicole, don't you have a cousin in the border patrol in Tucson?" Chase asked. "I don't know anyone there."

An exasperated sigh preceded Nicole's voice. "Yes. I'll ask about surveillance videos."

"Thanks, Nicole," Sam said. "I'll let you know if the sheriff provides anything useful, or if Jade miraculously shows up. Chase, you can take me off speaker now."

"We're off," Chase confirmed on the phone. "I'm walking out of the room now, leaving Nicole alone with this pile of fascinating bank statements."

After a beat, he said, "I'm sorry if it seemed like I wasn't taking you seriously. Where are you right now? Tell me you're not camped out by the wall."

"Not yet. I'm in Bisbee, trying to figure out my next step."

"You said Jade was taking a photo. Was it significant in some way? Did it by any chance include illegal activity or migrants?"

"No."

"This is about an animal, isn't it?" His tone made him sound remarkably like Jade's mother had on the phone last night, a mixture of disapproving and perplexed. Sam experienced a pang of kinship with her roommate.

She didn't want to share the jaguar with Chase yet. "It was an animal stopped by the wall, so it wouldn't be significant to most authorities. Jade only sent me that one photo, but I imagine she took a lot more, so I guess she could have observed something I don't know about. She's a professional photographer, and she usually doesn't shoot photos with her phone, either, unless it's some sort of emergency and she can't set up the photo properly with her camera. So I'm worried. And Maya keeps asking about her."

"Maya? Why?"

Sam realized she hadn't told Chase about the possible relationship of her two friends. She did it now.

He whistled softly. "That's an amazing coincidence."

"Isn't it? And now Jade has vanished."

"Poor Maya!"

"She doesn't know. I'm not telling her until I know what happened. So if she calls you—"

"I know nothing about anyone named Jade Silva."

"Thank you." After swallowing down the last of her iced tea, Sam confessed, "Chase, I found what looked like a big bloodstain in the middle of a bunch of footprints."

"Are you sure it's blood?"

"Reasonably."

"Where were these footprints?"

"Out in the middle of a brushy desert area."

"So . . . ?" He let the question hang in the air between them.

"The blood, if it is blood, could belong to almost anyone, or to an animal, too, I guess. But I'm worried that it might be Jade's or—"—she almost said *the jaguar's* but instead lamely concluded with— "—or someone else's."

"Let me know what the sheriff says. And I'll lean on Nicole to work her connections."

"Thanks, Chase. I've really missed hearing your voice."

"Me too. Are you really going to stay there for another month?"

"That's the plan. And you're way out on the Olympic Peninsula anyway, so it's not like you're missing me in your bed at the cabin. It's beautiful here at the station. These Sky Islands are amazing. I'm learning so much. I saw an elegant trogon yesterday."

The silence on his end lasted so long that she added, "That's a bird."

"I was debating between a butterfly and a lizard."

She laughed. "I miss you."

"Likewise," he murmured, his voice warm.

"Enjoy your time with Nicole."

"It's work, Summer," he reassured her. "And Nic's having a hard time. She and her husband might be separating."

Sam didn't know what to say. As long as she'd known Chase and his FBI partner, Nicole and her sculptor husband had been zooming off for romantic weekends, and the hubby had always sent her flowers and trinkets when Nicole was away on assignments. It was hard to believe that any man would dump elegant Nicole, unless it was the ugly need-a-younger-model crisis that so many successful men seemed to go through.

"That's terrible," Sam finally ventured, trying to sound sincere about the possible breakup and vanquish her concern about Chase with his oh-so-attractive and maybe now so available female partner. "I hope they work things out."

"Me too. But I'm glad she's here. If I have to analyze bank statements and interview accountants and bank clerks, it's nice to analyze and interview with someone I already trust and can laugh with."

"I understand," Sam said. *More or less.* Did Chase sound like he was having fun? "I was just beginning to have a relationship like that with Jade."

"I hope she's waiting for you when you get back to the research station."

"I'll email you if she is."

"Be careful, *querida.* The whole border area is a hot zone, and I'm not talking about climate."

"I know, Chase. It's dangerous for all the living creatures in it."

"This *is* about some animal, isn't it?"

He knew her too well. "And Jade."

Chase's sigh was audible over the airwaves. "Take care, Summer."

"I will. *Te quiero.*" She tapped the End Call icon.

After she finished her lunch, she used her phone to look up the location of the Cochise County Sheriff's Office. Which happened to be, conveniently, in Bisbee.

The drive there took less than ten minutes.

As Sam entered the lobby, a woman in uniform stood up and watched expectantly from behind bullet-proof glass panels at a front desk. Through a small opening in the glass, she asked, "Can I help you?"

Sam explained that she was trying to locate her roommate and needed to know whether Jade Silva had been involved in any incidents in the last thirty-six hours or so.

"Is she legal?" the woman asked. Her name tag indicated that she was D. Ortega.

Sam had only been in the area for a little more than two weeks, and she was already getting tired of the question. "Do you have to ask?"

"I only ask because if she's not and if she got picked up by the border patrol, her name might not be in our records."

*That's just great*, Sam thought. "Do you get asked about your citizenship all the time, Miss Ortega?"

"Deputy Ortega," the woman responded in a curt tone. "And the answer is no, not when I'm wearing my uniform."

Sam was tempted to ask what happened when D. Ortega was wearing jeans and a T-shirt. But judging by the annoyance reflected in the deputy's eyes, she needed to stay focused on her mission to locate one specific Hispanic-American woman. "Jade Silva is an American citizen."

"Let me check. It'll take a few minutes." Ortega plopped into a wheeled office chair in front of a computer, vanishing from Sam's view behind the monitor.

For a few minutes, Sam heard only the sounds of typing. Then Deputy Ortega appeared at the window again. "We have only an Oscar Silva in our records. Picked up for DUI in Douglas."

"So not even close?"

Ortega shook her head. "Not unless he's a relative. Do you want to file a missing person report?"

"What's your policy on that?"

Ortega explained that unless there were indications of foul play, the only result would be that deputies might keep an eye out for Jade's CR-V, providing that Sam had the license plate number.

Why hadn't she brought that information with her? She could picture her notes now, lying on her desk in the dorm room. "I don't have Jade's license plate number with me, but you could look that up, right?"

"You said she's from New Mexico," the deputy remarked.

"Right." *But you could still get that information,* she thought, but kept the notion to herself. What did she know? Maybe the states of New Mexico and Arizona refused to cooperate with each other. "I went to a place by the wall where I know Jade was last seen, but I couldn't find footprints. It seemed like the road there had been swept or smoothed out somehow."

The deputy nodded. "Border patrol periodically drags tires and stuff like that to wipe out any marks."

The question must have shown in Sam's face, because the deputy went on to explain. "So that when the sensors report that someone came over the border, the agents will have prints to follow."

Sam supposed that made sense, but it certainly didn't help in her search. "In one place, I did find a lot of footprints. Plus, torn clothing and punctured water bottles were everywhere, like there had been a big fight."

Ortega waved a dismissive hand in the air. "That proves nothing. The border patrol destroys migrants' belongings when they find them."

"What?" Sam stared at her. "Why?"

"To discourage the migrants. To make their journey more difficult."

Sam had to make an effort to relax her jaw. Destroying their clothes and water supplies certainly would make things more difficult for anyone hiking across the desert. No wonder migrants were dying out there. And the debris strewn across the landscape . . . No, she couldn't focus on that now, and there was no point in dwelling on how wrong it seemed.

"I found a big patch of what might be blood in the brush less than a mile away from the wall. I took a sample of that; I have it right here." She pulled the tissue roll from her pocket.

The look the deputy gave her was half pitying, half exasperated. "In this county, we have coyotes, both human and canine, and border patrol grabbing migrants, and migrants hurting themselves and each other, and legal hunters, and ranchers who have a right to protect their livestock—do I need to go on?"

Sam shook her head.

"We can't investigate every strange discovery in the desert," Ortega concluded. "And blood analysis is expensive."

"I thought there were field kits, at least to determine if it's blood and maybe to determine if it's human."

"Not here." The deputy gave her a stony stare.

"I get it." Chastised, Sam slipped the tissue wad back into her pocket.

Ortega folded her arms across her chest. "You don't even have any evidence that a crime has been committed."

"I understand," Sam reiterated, nodding to emphasize the point.

Picking up a pen from the counter, the deputy pointed it in Sam's direction. "Here's how it is. Competent adults have a right to their privacy. And you said this Jade is twenty-nine, didn't you? And you're not even a relative, am I right?"

Sam had to admit that she and Jade were not related.

"I suggest you contact your friend's actual relatives and other associates to find out if they've heard from her. And you might call the hospitals to see if she's been admitted anywhere."

"I'll do that, thanks." Sam put a hand on the counter and leaned forward. "Jade was last seen down by the wall," she said in a lower voice. "The border patrol would have video of everything that goes on down there, wouldn't they?"

Ortega rolled her eyes. "I really wouldn't know."

Stifling an irritated retort, Sam straightened. "Okay. Thank you for your help."

The deputy softened her stance. "I hope you find your friend."

*Me too*, Sam thought. Back in her car, she called the office at the Southwestern Research Station.

"No, we haven't seen or heard from Jade," the assistant director told her.

Sam heard the murmur of voices in the background, then, "Hang on just a moment; I've got someone here who wants to talk to you."

Bev's booming voice was next. "Hi, Sam. Where are you?"

"Bisbee."

"So you can get back in around ninety minutes? That's a little late for the prep, but I really need your help with dinner."

*But I'm not on the list for volunteer duty*, Sam felt like whining. She realized that odds were good that Jade's name was on the roster. And her disappointment had more to do with not finding any sign of Jade's whereabouts than with being shanghaied for dinner duty.

*Free room and board in a beautiful place*, she reminded herself. Plus, she needed to finish her article for Save the Wilderness. The deadline for the next issue was tomorrow.

"Please?" Bev herself sounded close to whining.

"I'm going to make a few phone calls, then I'm on my way."

Sitting on the bench outside in the shade, Sam spent twenty minutes looking up hospitals across the county and the two neighboring counties, then calling them. None had admitted Jade Silva in the last two days.

Admitting defeat, at least for the day, Sam headed east and then north to the research station and kitchen duties.

# 8

When there was still no sign of Jade after dinner, Sam used her video-chat app to call Chase and report her findings. Except for the Navajo Nation, Arizona did not observe daylight savings time, so the hour was the same in Washington State. Chase answered on his phone. Judging by all the neon decorations and chiming noises in the background, he was clearly in a restaurant or bar inside the casino.

Smiling, he crooned, *"Mi amor. Qué pasa?"*

"I still miss you, Chase."

"Likewise. Even though we spoke only hours ago." He was not wearing a tie, a signal that he was not officially on duty at the moment.

"Want me to hang up?" she asked.

"Never. I never get enough of you. It's nice to see your face."

"I'm surrounded by people here, but I'm lonely," she confided. "I feel like Don Quixote."

"Jousting at windmills? Traveling in a dream world?"

"Maybe the windmill part. Dream world, I wish; I'm ready to wake up. I guess I don't feel like Don Quixote, then. I don't know who I feel like, but I seem to be the only one who cares that Jade might be in trouble."

"The operative word being 'might'?"

"Granted, I don't know Jade well, but it's not normal for anyone to just vanish, is it?" She told him about her frustrating visit to the sheriff's office and her unproductive calls to local hospitals. "I hope someone would worry about me if I simply dropped out of sight."

"I'd search heaven and earth for you, Summer."

"Thanks, Starchaser."

"Eventually," he added, grinning. "You've been known to go off on a tangent or two yourself, you know. Utah, Ecuador, the Olympics, the North Cascades . . ."

"Those were jobs," she protested. "I knew what I was doing. Well, most of the time, anyway. But Jade, at the wall . . . anything could have happened."

His gaze slid sideways and then back to the screen. "Hang on. Nicole may have something for you."

Sam was irritated that apparently Nicole had been at the table during her whole conversation with Chase. Catching a glance of her scowl in the wall mirror across the dorm room, she focused on smoothing the frown lines from her brow before Nicole's face appeared on the screen.

In spite of the fact that she wore a casual striped blouse open at the neck, Agent Boudreaux was, unnaturally, impeccably neat. Her auburn hair was parted on the side and chin length, cut with a razor-sharp edge, and tucked behind an ear that was tastefully decorated with a small blue opal earring.

"Hi, Nicole." Sam squelched the urge to run her fingers over her own hair and finger her earlobes to see if she'd even remembered to put on earrings this morning. "How are you?"

"Summer," was Nicole's only word of greeting. "As Chase so thoughtfully remembered, my cousin works in surveillance in the border patrol office, but in Bisbee, not Tucson. She found a clip that might be of interest. She can meet you tomorrow at five p.m. in Bisbee. I'll text you her name and address. Bring a laptop."

Sam checked the volunteer schedule she'd taped to the wall. She was on the roster tomorrow for dinner duty. Another volunteer, Jim Hipp, was scheduled for lunch. She'd convince him to swap with her. "I'll make that work."

"Don't tell anyone you're meeting with her."

"Thanks, Nicole."

Nicole's blue-eyed gaze was piercing, even on the computer screen. "This conversation never happened."

"Got it." Sam worked to keep her gaze just as steely.

The secrecy of government agencies was annoying. Most seemed to regard the information they collected as collateral to be guarded at all costs from the public. Sometimes it seemed like the government operated more "against the people" instead of "for the people" or "of the people."

"Here's Chase." Nicole slid out of view, and the phone briefly displayed a view of dim ceiling lights.

"Thanks, Nicole!" Sam said loudly, hoping Chase's partner could still hear.

The next afternoon, Sam drove to Bisbee to discover that Nicole's cousin looked nothing like the FBI agent. Maria Gage was broad-shouldered, plump, and brown-haired, with a sprinkle of freckles across her nose. As soon as Sam stepped out of her RAV4 in front of a frumpy apartment building, Maria was there to shake her hand and take her laptop case.

"So glad you could come," Maria said. "I really hope you can help me out with all this tax stuff."

*Tax stuff?* "My pleasure," Sam said uncertainly.

Maria led her to door number 7. Once inside, Nicole's cousin leaned back on the door, handed the laptop case back to Sam, and gestured to the table in the dining area. "You never know who's watching or listening in Bisbee," Maria explained. "You're a bookkeeper friend who has come to help me make sense of my receipts and such."

Sam snorted. "I could use a friend like that, myself." She slid into a chair.

Maria remained standing on the opposite side of the table. "I don't know why we're not supposed to share information with citizens like you."

"I suppose it's in case I'm a drug kingpin who is trying to find out what you know. Or maybe that should be a queenpin?"

Maria laughed. "You're not either, are you?"

"What I know about the drug business can be etched on the head of a pin." She opened her laptop.

"But seriously," Maria warned, tapping the table with a fingertip, "if you ever mention this to anyone, I'll turn you in as a hacker, and that's a federal offense."

"Whoa!" Sam held up both hands. "You can trust me, Maria. I know you're doing me a favor. I'm simply trying to find a friend who disappeared a couple of days ago down by the border wall between Douglas and Naco."

"That's what Nic said. A new red Honda CR-V, right?" The plump woman moved to a small desk along the wall and retrieved a small green USB drive from a drawer.

"Right." Sam powered up her laptop.

"Okay." Maria plugged the thumb drive into a port on the side of Sam's computer. "This is only a short clip and it's pretty dark, but I think it shows the vehicle you're looking for."

She sat in a chair beside Sam, pulled the laptop toward herself, then brought up the video and adjusted the angle so Sam could view it.

The image was dark and grainy. The timestamp said 6:13 a.m. Less than an hour after Jade sent that photo. At first there was nothing on the screen but a wide-angle view of a gravel

road and the surrounding brushy hills, but then an SUV drove
into view. As it came broadside to the camera, Sam could see
that it was a CR-V and could be a dark-red color. She couldn't
make out the driver, but as the vehicle passed the camera, she
could see that it had a bumper sticker on the back. The license
plate was a blur.

Maria pointed. "Is that it? Your friend's CR-V?"

"I think so."

The vehicle drove out of view to the left of the screen.
Shortly afterward, a car zipped into view, going the same
direction. Or more accurately, a cloud of dust rolled across the
screen. Sam couldn't tell anything beyond the fact that the
vehicle was a sedan, not an SUV, and that it was a dark color.
She wondered how the driver could see, driving so close
behind the CR-V.

Then a reddish glow brightened the left side of the screen.
"Taillights?" Sam guessed.

"Probably. One of those vehicles most likely stopped just
out of view."

Then a white light entered the video from the opposite
side. The reddish glow on the left side of the screen went out. A
border patrol SUV drove into view from the right, then quickly
passed down the road. The video ended.

"Is that it?" Sam asked, disappointed.

"That's it," Maria said. "That's all I found. There's another
camera in the area, but it was out of commission."

"Really? Do the bad guys disable them or something?

Maria's lips twitched. "I guess that sometimes 'bad
guys'"—she made air quotes—"might attempt to break one, but
mostly it's just weather or rodents chewing the wires or
something. Or sometimes a hawk or an eagle nests on top of
the solar panel, and there goes the power. The wall's the
priority right now. Maintenance on towers, not so much. Even

maintenance on the wall, not so much."

"Maintenance on the wall?" The sections she'd seen had looked like it would take a tank to ram them down. "What's to maintain?"

"Sometimes migrants try to tunnel under. But mostly, people cut holes in some sections."

"What?" Sam was incredulous.

"Yep. It's not so hard; just rent a blowtorch and . . ." Maria made a hissing sound as she went through the motions of cutting out a square. "Bolt cutters take longer, but they work on the sections with mesh, too. I hear that in California, people were cutting out circles for barbeque grills." She shrugged. "They might still be, for all I know."

"Huh. I guess that's American ingenuity. Or maybe Mexican." Sam focused again on her laptop. "Where was this video taken?"

"I'll show you." Maria moved back to the desk and extracted a map from a cubbyhole. Flattening it across the dining table, she pointed. "This is the access road in the video. The vehicles were traveling north."

Sam frowned. What did it mean? Did the video prove *anything*? "Can I watch it again?"

"Watch it as many times as you like. I'm getting a beer." Maria headed for the refrigerator. "You want a beer?"

"No, thanks." Inhabiting the land of brewpubs had ruined Sam's taste for any beer that wasn't on tap. "I've got to drive back to Portal tonight."

She watched the video three more times. She was reasonably certain that the gravel road in the video was the same access road she'd encountered just after finding the red stain in the dirt. The pattern of the brushy hills in the background appeared familiar, too. But no matter how hard she squinted, she couldn't identify the CR-V driver or the license plate on the back. The sedan remained a dusty blur. The license plate on the border patrol vehicle was not visible, either, but the white SUV had green letters and numbers on the back of it. "You can identify this patrol truck, right?" she asked. "The driver might have seen Jade."

"It's assigned to Agent Landon Imhoff."

"How could I find him?"

Maria forced a laugh, but her tone was bitter. "If you locate him, you should contact the main office in Tucson ASAP."

Sam shifted her gaze from her laptop screen to the woman leaning on the kitchen counter.

"Imhoff is MIA." Maria took a swig from her beer bottle. "Don't tell anyone I said that."

"Did something happen to him?"

Maria shrugged. "They found his SUV late last night in a grocery store lot in Douglas. His duty belt and other equipment were inside. But nobody's seen Imhoff himself for more than forty eight hours."

Sam sat back in the chair. "What do you think happened? Is he okay?"

"We all hope so. So far, there's no sign of him. We don't think it's a cartel thing." She took another swallow of beer. "They're usually not subtle. They'd leave Imhoff's body, or at least some part of it, in plain view in his vehicle if they were trying to send a message."

Sam winced.

"Imhoff was only twenty-two," Maria said. "And he'd only been on the job for sixteen months. It's not uncommon for the young ones to quit early on." She took another sip. "It's a little odd to walk away with no notice, though."

"I'd really like to talk to him."

"You and everyone else. His supervisors and buddies have

been calling around everywhere. He hasn't contacted family or friends, and he hasn't been back to his apartment in Douglas."

He walked away with nothing? What could have happened? She thought back to Jade's mother's comments about Jade's lovers, which included *Lenny or Lanny something, somewhere near the Arizona border.* "Maria, did you say Imhoff's first name was Landon?"

"That's right. Why? Do you know him?"

"No." Sam shook her head. Could Agent Imhoff and Jade be together somewhere? Had they planned to run off? An ugly thought crossed her mind, based on Chase's past history of working undercover in the southwest. "Could Imhoff be . . ." She struggled to find the right word.

"Dirty?" Maria guessed. Shrugging again, she said, "We've had a few who've gone to the dark side. When you're making peanuts and stationed in the middle of nowhere, it's hard to resist an offer to live like royalty in Mexico."

Or, Sam thought, maybe Imhoff had already been working for a cartel, and Jade had been in the wrong place at the wrong time. Maybe she'd seen something she shouldn't have. Now Sam had more questions than ever, but maybe she had a clue to follow. Landon Imhoff, missing border patrol agent.

She pointed to the USB drive. "Can I keep this? I'll be glad to pay . . ."

Maria strode quickly over and yanked the drive out of the laptop port. "No way. And I never showed it to you. Or told you about Imhoff." She slid the thumb drive into the back pocket of her jeans. "Remember what I said about the hacking."

"I understand." Sam stood up. "Thank you, Maria." She pulled her business card from her pocket. "If Officer Imhoff shows up, could you let me know?"

"I will if I can. I hope you find your friend."

"Jade Silva, that's her name."

"It's dangerous down here for women. Especially young Hispanic women. Watch yourself."

"Likewise."

After Sam had bundled up her laptop, Nicole's cousin walked her to the parking lot. As Sam opened the door of her RAV4, she said aloud, "So Maria, I think you've got it now, right? Just keep the receipts organized and you'll have no trouble."

Maria winked. "Organization doesn't come naturally to me, but I'll try, girlfriend."

# 9

Before returning to the station, Sam grabbed a sandwich and a bottle of orange juice at a convenience store in Douglas. Sitting at one of the two tables outside in the parking lot, she took advantage of available cell phone coverage to call the Douglas border patrol station and ask for Agent Landon Imhoff.

"He can't be reached right now; he's in the field," the receptionist told her.

She chewed another bite of her sandwich. What had she expected? That the border patrol would admit one of the agents was MIA?

"Do you have a message for him? I can make sure it gets to his in-box."

"I'll catch up with him later," Sam lied. "But hey, I wrote down his cell number wrong. I can't read my own handwriting. I think this says 530 . . ."

"The area code for Douglas is 520," the receptionist told her.

"Okay, so this should be 520 . . ."

When Sam paused, the receptionist said, "The border patrol doesn't give out personal information about employees."

"But I'm his girlfriend!" Sam lied.

"Then you should have that information."

"It was worth a try," she told the dial tone. After

swallowing the last of the dry sandwich, she washed it down with a final gulp of orange juice.

Hoping that the 520 area code was a hint, Sam pulled up a website on her phone and typed in Landon Imhoff Douglas AZ. Zilch. She tried the Cochise County Assessor's site, found an Imhoff on Carmelita Avenue in Douglas. Setting her phone to GPS mode, she followed its instructions to find the address. It was only seven thirty, she excused herself, not too late to knock on doors.

Maria said that the agent was only twenty-two. If she was going to try to pass for a friend of his, it was probably best not to look like his mother. Scraping her hair up into a messy ponytail, Sam tried to alter her appearance to be at least a little closer to late twenties than to her true decade older.

The man who answered her knock had to be at least sixty. He was only few inches taller than Sam's five one, and his round face reminded Sam of a garden gnome. "I'm looking for Landon?"

"You and everyone else," he groused. "That boy had better show up soon."

She'd prepared a cover story in the car. "I loaned him a DVD of a movie, and I really need it back."

His bushy brows crawled toward the crease above his nose as he eyed her, as if trying to guess her relationship to his son. In the living room behind him, she could see tall shelves filled with books.

"The DVD belongs to the library," she improvised. "I'm a volunteer there, and there are twenty-eight people waiting for it."

"Go see Naomi in the apartment, then." He tilted his head toward a detached garage, and now Sam noticed a stairway up the side of that building to the second floor. "She might be able to find it for you."

"Thanks!" She flounced off toward the garage. Or at least she tried to flounce; that seemed to be what someone closer to twenty-two would do.

A young woman answered the door, her belly preceding the rest of her. The poor thing appeared to be eleven months pregnant. Her pale brown hair was lank, and her eyes were red as if she'd been crying. Sam felt guilty for making her stand upright as she explained, "Hi, I'm a friend of Landon's from work. Well, actually, I'm more of a friend of a friend. I told Jade Silva I'd do this favor for her. Do you know Jade?"

"No." The pregnant woman sounded as if she were exhausted, and she sagged against the door frame. "I don't understand. How do you know Landon?"

Sam giggled. "I don't, really. Jade does. This is her." She held out the phone, showing her roommate's photo.

The woman studied the screen for a minute. "How does Jade know Landon?"

The woman's eyes had registered no recognition, so she'd probably never seen Jade. "I think they met at the library," Sam hedged, continuing the theme.

"When was this?" Landon's wife, or girlfriend, or baby mama, seemed to be getting suspicious. Or maybe she was trying to find clues of her own.

"Anyhow," Sam detoured from the subject, "Jade said she loaned Landon a DVD, and she needs it back. It belongs to the library."

The woman winced and clutched her stomach with both hands as if fondling a beachball. "He's kicking a lot today."

"That has to be uncomfortable."

"It is. I'm a week overdue." When her eyes met Sam's again, she asked, "Can I have this Jade's phone number? Maybe she knows where he is?"

Reaching behind her, she magically pulled out a cell phone from what must have been a back pocket.

"Uh," Sam stuttered. She really wasn't good at this. "I don't have Jade's number with me."

"Then maybe I could have yours?"

"Sure." Sam rattled off her cell number, changing the last two digits.

The woman punched it in. "So I'll call you later, and you can get Jade's number for me."

"Sure," Sam said again. "And you're—? So I know who's calling?"

"I'm Naomi Kelso, Landon's fiancée." She put special emphasis on the last word. Stepping to the side, she pointed to a photo on the entryway wall. The man with his arm around Naomi was also young, with light-brown hair and a thin mustache. In the photo, she was holding out her hand toward the camera, showing off the ring.

Naomi moved back to her previous position, blocking Sam's view of the engagement photo. "Have *you* heard from Landon in the last couple of days?" she asked.

"Nope," Sam responded. "But like I said, I really don't know him, so why would he call me? He's with the border patrol, right? Is he on duty now?"

The woman's sad blue eyes were fixed in Sam's direction, but her gaze seemed unfocused. "Supposed to be."

This conversation was going nowhere fast. Sam moved toward the stairway. "Well, I'd better be going. Sorry to bother you."

"What about the DVD?"

"You look like you need to sit down." Or lie down. Or give birth within the next half hour. "I don't want to make you find it now. I've decided it's Jade's problem. Talk to you later, Naomi."

As she trudged down the wooden staircase, she felt remorse for her pretense. Naomi was in a worse position than she was, searching for a missing person. Or, more likely, *waiting* for her missing fiancé; the poor girl was in no condition to actually *search* for anyone.

The only information she'd gained was that the missing border patrol agent had a pregnant fiancée, and that the fiancée did not know Jade. But that proved nothing. Jade and Landon might have never met, and had simply vanished at the same time out of coincidence.

Or Jade and Landon could have run off together and might be having wild, bunny-humping sex somewhere in an out-of-the-way motel. Sam hoped that was the case; it was the least bad possibility she could think of.

No, not the least bad. There could still be a good outcome for both missing people. Maybe Landon would simply show up tonight, having overcome an attack of anxiety about marriage and fatherhood. Maybe Jade would show up tonight, too, after dealing with a car problem or after chasing that jaguar for two days. But each hour that ticked by left Sam with a heavier weight of dread in her gut.

In the hour it took to drive back to the station, Sam thought about how badly she missed Chase. And Simon. And Blake. And Maya. Oh jeez, Maya. The teen would call again tonight. She'd already left dozens of messages.

# 10

The next day, after her breakfast volunteer duties, Sam drove south and west along the border road. She was apparently driving too slowly for local tastes, because a pickup passed her, headed west, its doors emblazoned with the name of MacGregor Ranch. Two plumy tails streamed out the back of the horse trailer the truck was pulling. Sam felt sorry for the horses enclosed in the metal structure on a hot day, but maybe the breeze kept them cool enough. Next came an extended-cab pickup with two men in cowboy hats in the front seat. She couldn't see who rode in the back, but the rifles hanging against the rear window were alarming. She counted four weapons in the rack.

Way too many guns riding around down here, just as Diego Xintal had said.

She finally turned north on the gravel access road that Jade's CR-V had followed in the video, watching closely for the boulder she'd marked. There—was that it? She braked to a stop and pulled out her binoculars. Yes, there was a faint X etched into the rock. Sliding out of the SUV, she surveyed the area, trying to put herself in Jade's shoes. She walked to the marked boulder, then moved out in a semicircle, her eyes on the ground. Yes, the scrap of blue cloth fluttering from the nearby bush seemed familiar. And there was the darker patch of dirt.

It had faded substantially since two days ago, but this was the place.

She examined the paw print again, and ambled slowly in the direction that it indicated. The hard-packed dirt between the bushes revealed little, but she thought some scrape marks might have been made by a jaguar's paw. Or the toe of a sneaker. Or the heel of a boot. She continued the search for nearly an hour, but she was simply not a good enough tracker to identify the signs, if there were any, of a big cat passing through this dry scrub country. Too many people had traveled through this area recently to sort out all the partial shoe prints.

Based on what she'd learned about his jaguar research, Diego Xintal must have superior tracking skills. She made a mental note to confer with him.

Had her roommate tracked the jaguar from the wall and then stopped her CR-V just beyond the reach of the surveillance camera to follow the cat on foot? In Jade's photo, the jaguar looked as if he were considering leaping into the concertina wire looped across the top of the wall. If he had tried to scale the wall, the blood was most likely his. Maybe Jade had stopped to help the animal. Maybe she'd taken him to a vet somewhere. But unless the big cat was mortally wounded, capturing him didn't seem possible without tranquilizer darts, and as far as Sam knew, Jade didn't pack those.

Maybe the border patrol agent, Imhoff, had stopped to help her. Maybe he had tranquilizer darts. Or a Taser and a net, or something.

Damn. So many maybes.

It was annoying that with surveillance cameras on towers and drones buzzing overhead, no more video had been caught of Jade's car or of Imhoff's border patrol vehicle. If there was as much traffic on the gravel access road as that homeowner,

Carl Straub, had complained about, it seemed like *someone* should have seen *something*.

Sam walked back to her car and then drove slowly up the access road to the north, passing the Straubs' driveway. A winding dirt path led to a dilapidated wooden shack tilting sideways in the distance. If Jade were injured or stranded on foot, might she have taken refuge there? After parking the RAV4, Sam walked to the building. With windows broken out and no door visible in the front opening, the structure appeared to be abandoned, but as she approached, she called out, "Hello? Anyone here?"

When there was no response, she dared to stick her head inside.

Nobody was inside, but people had clearly stopped here. The floor was littered with a crushed gallon-size plastic water bottle, a red toy dinosaur, a bent prayer card with an image of a saint, as well as a pile of stained clothing spread out, as if someone had used it as a makeshift bed. Sam stared at the intermingled fabrics, trying to remember Jade's clothing. She hadn't seen how her roommate was dressed when she'd slipped out, but they each had only a few items of clothing hanging from the rods in their room. Didn't Jade have a green plaid shirt like that piece of fabric there? And were her eyes playing tricks, or was it *moving*?

She froze as a forked tongue emerged, followed by a spade-shaped snake's head with its unblinking eyes. Then the entire body slid out in front of Sam's hiking boots. The distinctive skin pattern and buttons on its tail marked it as a rattlesnake. Her breath caught in her throat as it slithered toward her feet. She didn't want to think about what would happen if the snake bit her here, many miles away from medical help.

She willed herself to stay absolutely still. After a brief

taste-test of the air around her ankles that made her heart skip a beat, the rattlesnake serpentined its way toward the sunlight spilling in from the doorway.

When she had counted to ten, Sam chanced a glance over her right shoulder. The snake was no longer in view. She exhaled a long slow breath and shook out her hands and arms, trying to release the rigor that had seized her entire body. She prayed the snake was not waiting just outside the door. As a wildlife biologist, she recognized the ecological value of snakes, especially as predators of rodents, but she'd never determined why some needed to be so venomous to fit into the web of life.

Gingerly, she nudged the green fabric with the toe of her boot. It seemed to be a shirt or part of one, spotted with dark-brown stains and twisted among other pieces of clothing in the pile. After seeing the rattler, Sam had no intention of investigating them further. Who knew what might be coiled up beneath them?

She scrutinized the small structure. The child's toy and the prayer card seemed sad; she hoped the owners of the items were alive and well, wherever they were. A small silver earring lay in the dirt next to the wall. Sam picked it up. It was a small hoop for a pierced ear, and it was not particularly distinctive. It might not even be real silver. She tried to remember whether Jade had a pair like it. Maybe, maybe not. She slipped it into her pocket.

After moving to the doorway, she peered out cautiously. She saw no sign of the rattlesnake, but kept a wary eye on the ground as she walked back to her car. Just as she approached her RAV4, a border patrol SUV drove past, slowing as the agent inside scrutinized her from head to toe. He must have decided that she was no threat, because he waved and sped onward, and she was grateful to have pale skin and blond hair. Only seconds later, that gratitude made her feel dirty, like she'd joined a white supremacist movement.

Sam continued her journey north, scanning both sides of the access road as she drove. On the west side, she soon encountered a huge parking lot surrounded by a high chain-link fence topped with strands of taut barbed wire. Inside the lot were several trucks, a flatbed like the one she'd seen two days ago, this one with a small crane chained to its bed; a monster utility truck with a large winch on its front; and a half-dozen giant heavy-duty pickups. The sign next to the gate read RTK CONSTRUCTION.

The double gate was wide open, so she drove in. Choosing between two one-story buildings, she parked in front of the one that looked most like an office.

After pocketing her cell phone, she pulled the front door open and walked inside, welcoming the embrace of air conditioning that wafted around her. The desk in the reception area was vacant, but through an open doorway she saw several men grouped around a table. It sounded as though they were all speaking Spanish. Her watch showed only 10:20 a.m., but if these guys started their work before dawn as Carl Straub had said, she supposed this could be their lunch hour.

A large man with a dark tan, a thick handlebar mustache, and sweat stains on the armpits of his denim cowboy shirt stood up from his chair when he spotted her in the doorway. "Can I help you, ma'am?" A half-eaten sandwich dangled from his right hand.

She stepped inside the tile-floored room, which held five small, round tables surrounded by a multitude of cheap plastic chairs. One side of the room was dedicated to a long countertop with a double sink, flanked by trash bins. A coffee maker anchored one end of the counter, and a huge refrigerator filled the corner.

All the men—she counted six—were examining her curiously.

"Sorry to interrupt, guys. I just wanted to ask a question." Gesturing to the standing man, she said, "Please sit and finish your lunch."

He seemed reluctant, but slid back into his chair. She inserted herself at the side of the table between two of the men, trying not to wrinkle her nose at the strong odor of sweat emanating from the crew. After introducing herself, she explained that she was trying to locate someone who might have been near the wall several days ago. "A young Hispanic woman."

Bringing up Jade's photo on her phone, she held it out, showing it slowly to each of the six men. "She was driving a new red CR-V."

One of the other men whistled. She glanced at him, unsure whether his reaction was to the photo of Jade or to the description of her vehicle. Grinning, he glanced around the table. "*Una chica rica.*"

"*Bonita, también,*" another offered.

"Jade Silva *is* pretty," Sam answered to demonstrate she understood a modicum of Spanish, thanks to Chase. "But she's not rich. She works hard for her money."

The two men had the good grace to look embarrassed. Fixing their gaze on the meals in front of them, they returned to eating.

"Did any of you spot her or her car? She was last seen by the wall three days ago."

All six of the men at the table shook their heads.

She turned to the mustachioed man who had stood up. "Are you the boss?"

Swiveling in his seat, he held out a calloused hand. "Ryan Ramirez. I'm the *R* in RTK. Ramirez, Thorensen, and Kidd."

*Thorensen.* "Did I see that name, Thorensen, on the wall?"

Ramirez's mustache twitched. "Yeah, it's there. So's mine. And Kidd's. We all do that sometimes, mark our work." He shrugged. "Reminds people who's really building this wall."

He sounded proud of the work. She wanted to ask him how he and his crew, obvious Hispanics whose family members most likely had been immigrants at some point, felt about putting up a barricade to keep other immigrants out. But remembering how Deputy Ortega had bristled when asked that flavor of question, she decided to stay mum on that for the moment. Instead, she asked, "When will all the crews come back? I'd like to ask them about my friend, too."

Ramirez shrugged again. "I couldn't say. It depends on the weather and when they started, and if the border patrol or the army engineers are there, lookin' over their shoulders. Different employees go out and come back at different times, depending on whether they're building or repairing fence."

Engines briefly rumbled outside, then shut down. The wheeze of the hydraulic closer on the front door preceded another group of men who tramped into the building.

"Here's another of our crews." Ramirez stood up again. "Guys, this woman wants to show you a photo and ask if you've seen her friend or a red SUV."

"CR-V," Sam clarified, holding out her phone with Jade's photo as the eight men passed through the doorway. Each paused, studied the photo for a minute, then shook his head before heading for the sink to wash his hands. The stench of sweat in the room intensified.

"Thanks for the information, Mr. Ramirez, and the rest of you," she told them all. "I guess I need to stop by at a later time to talk to the other crew. My friend went missing three days ago. Do you all remember if all your employees were working in this area then?"

Brushing his finger across his mustache, Ramirez thought for a second. "I'd have to check the timesheets."

"I covered for Phil," volunteered a dark-haired young man with sunglasses pushed to the top of his head. "He was out making sales calls, so he didn't show up early afternoon." After wiping his hands dry with a paper towel, he extended the clean fingers of his right hand toward her. "I'm David Muñoz. Say, you know anyone interested in a job? Needs to be good with numbers."

The front door wheezed open again, and a tall man in a straw cowboy hat preceded a man with red hair into the building, saying to him over his shoulder, "I just got a report of another hole; same sector as yesterday."

"We'll get down there after lunch," the redhead promised.

"Shit," the cowboy-hatted man groused. "Has it ever been this effin' hot in May before?"

"Phil, you say that every year." The woman who emerged from behind the two men was dressed in casual jeans and a sleeveless, button-down blouse, but somehow on her, they appeared expensive. Her layered, shoulder-length chestnut hair had strategically placed sun streaks. The rock on the woman's finger and the heavy Navajo silver and turquoise necklace at her throat was probably worth thousands.

"Speak of the devil . . ." Ramirez murmured.

The redhead slid around the other two people and strolled toward the sink. The remaining man and woman stared curiously at Sam. Then the man yanked off his cowboy hat, exposing gray hair matted against his head. "Who have we here?"

"We were just talking about you," Ramirez told the gray-haired man. "This is Summer Westin." As another group of men entered, he added, "And this here's our third crew. Miz Westin, this is Phil Thorensen."

As the first group of men stood up from the table, Sam held out her hand to Thorensen. He stared at it for a second before grasping her fingers gently with the tips of his own, then turned to include the woman. "This is my wife, Dulcie."

"I'm pleased to meet you." After shaking hands with the woman, Sam dropped her right hand to her side and handed Thorensen her phone with her left. "I'm trying to find this woman."

Lowering his head, Thorensen regarded the photo on the phone, squinting in concentration. His wife shifted into position beside him. He tilted the phone so she could view Jade's photo as well.

Sam told them, "I know she was down by the wall three days ago. She drives a red Honda CR-V. I wondered whether anyone here had noticed her or the vehicle?"

A group of incoming men flowed around them, moving toward the sink and refrigerator. The room was crowded now, and although the first group had vacated their table and were filtering out through the front door, the place still smelled like a locker room after a football game. Sam could almost taste the dirt and sweat. She wasn't sure how much longer she could stand the fug that permeated the atmosphere.

It seemed as if Thorensen's wife was feeling the same way, because Dulcie put a hand to her throat, looking as if she might vomit.

Phil Thorensen watched Dulcie, his brow wrinkled with concern. Wrapping an arm around her shoulders, he squeezed, giving her a sideways hug. "My wife's got a soft spot for lost souls."

Glancing up from the phone, Dulcie shook her head. "Sorry. I haven't seen her." Then she raised a manicured hand, curled her fingers into a fist in front of her lips, and sniffed before saying, "I shouldn't let it get to me like this. But it does, every time. She looks like so many of the others. It's just so sad. So many of them have died in the desert this year. Why do they keep coming?"

Desperation, Sam wanted to suggest. Poverty. Hopelessness. Fear. Or maybe something as simple as losing a job when a factory closed on the Mexican side of the border? She tried not to dwell on all the possibilities; they made her feel guilty just for being born in the United States. "She's just missing, not dead." Sam prayed her words were true.

Thorensen handed back Sam's phone. "Is that woman . . . uh . . . legal?" He raised watery blue eyes to meet Sam's gaze.

"Yes. Her name's Jade Silva. She's not a migrant. She's from Santa Fe."

"I just ask, because, well, you know." He shrugged. "Some who don't have papers are kinda here today and gone tomorrow, if you know what I mean."

"I do."

Jade *was* legal, wasn't she? Sam hadn't actually discussed that with Jade's mother, but neither Katerina Franco nor Jade had the slightest hint of a Hispanic accent, so Sam had assumed Katerina had been born and raised in the US, along with her daughter.

A younger man in a baseball cap sporting the logo of the Arizona Diamondbacks sidled up to them. "Here's Charlie Kidd," Thorensen introduced him. "Miz Westin here is looking for the girl in the picture on her phone."

She swiveled the phone toward Kidd, and he took it from her hand.

Blowing an air kiss toward Jade's image, Kidd then groaned, "Oh, come to me, *nena*." He seemed reluctant to hand back the phone. "I haven't seen her," he told Sam, "but I'd like to."

Apparently the 'me too' movement hadn't reached RTK Construction.

Dulcie Thorensen blew a puff of exasperation through her lips. "Oh, grow up, Charlie." She headed to the refrigerator.

Raising his chin, Kidd indicated the group of men washing at the sink. "Feel free to show that to all the guys."

All the workers denied seeing Jade. She returned to the cluster of partners. "Thanks for letting me ask around."

Ramirez looked at Thorensen and Kidd. "I was telling Miz Westin here about the accounting job." He turned back to her. "Ever done construction bids?"

"You're still bidding on wall construction?" she asked.

She'd heard that the border wall was costing an average of two million dollars per linear mile. In reality, no wall could follow the actual border, which was nearly two thousand miles long and snaked up mountains and threaded through canyons with sheer cliffs that dropped into rivers. But even if the whole thing was never constructed, the cost would be astronomical. She didn't want to think about what average Americans were giving up to pay for it.

"We do a lot more than just build the wall." Kidd pushed his baseball cap back on his head. "We make repairs, we put up housing for all the incoming patrol guys."

Thorensen added, "We're the facilitators down here. We can supply SUVs and surveillance stuff. Lights, generators, outbuildings."

Ramirez chimed in, joining their circle. "Sometimes we even arrange for food services and laundry facilities for the border patrol agents. We're the Arizona experts on the border area. Whatever the patrol or the army guys need, we get it for 'em. So if you know someone looking for anything, send 'em to us. We're working on a deal to build a new detention facility." He folded his arms across his chest.

"Speaking of which . . ." Kidd focused on Thorensen. "Is that deal with Xtel a go? Do we have a signed contract?"

Thorensen looked uncomfortable. "Their sales manager wasn't there when we showed up last Friday, so we had to reschedule. We're meeting tomorrow."

"Okay," Kidd said, "But we'll be dead in the water if we can't get that equipment in a few weeks."

Kidd faced Sam again. "If you know anyone who's looking for work, tell them that the job is never boring and the pay's never been better. You don't even have to find a place to live if you don't already have one. That building out back is our dormitory. Showers, big-screen TV, your own private bathroom. You interested in that accounting job, by any chance?"

She smiled at the three partners. "That sounds attractive, but I've never done bids or bookkeeping. I can barely balance my checkbook." Not to mention, she couldn't imagine baking in the oven of this Arizona desert and helping erect an unnatural barrier that would stop all living creatures.

"Don't nag the poor woman," Phil Thorensen told Ramirez. "Can't you see she's not interested?"

"Shame." Ramirez dropped his arms back to his sides. "Business has never been better, but it's hard to keep good employees."

"Do they find other jobs, or do they get deported?" Sam asked.

The expression that slid onto Ramirez's face made her regret the question as soon as the words were out of her mouth. He frowned, his heavy brows dipping into a vee.

*Please excuse Sam,* her housemate, Blake, would have remarked right now. *She was born with foot-in-mouth disease.*

Turning to Thorensen, she attempted to excuse herself.

"It's just you said here today, gone tomorrow, so ...'"
Watching hostility grow on the faces of both Thorensen and
Ramirez, she let her words trail off.

*Need a shovel to dig that hole a little deeper?* Blake's
voice asked in her head.

His voice sharp edged, Kidd said, "RTK doesn't hire
illegals."

"I see." Sam edged toward the door. "I'd better be going."

Ramirez took a step toward her. "Our employees have all
the appropriate paperwork. We are doing legitimate business
here and working damn hard for our money. We are securing
the border and enforcing the law."

Most of the men in the room were unabashedly staring at
her now. The odor and heat from the crush of male bodies
seemed to increase exponentially by the second. Even Dulcie,
who had taken a seat at a vacant table, briefly lifted her eyes
from the packaged salad in front of her.

Sam bit her lip. Why couldn't she ever stop herself from
wading into controversial quicksand?

"I understand. It was nice to meet you all." She nodded
nervously, feeling like a bobblehead doll. "Thank you for your
time." With a final small wave in Dulcie's direction, she fled
from the building.

The parking lot had filled with dusty white trucks of all
dimensions, along with one sedan, a metallic-green Audi. She
found her RAV4 wedged between a flatbed carrying two huge
generators and a pickup full of wire spools. It took four
creative turns to get out of the equipment maze. As she drove
out of the lot, Sam chewed her bottom lip.

How many men had been in the RTK lunchroom? That
must have been what Carl Straub had meant by *Half the locals
are in on it, lining their pockets.* The taco truck was probably
only one of many food-delivery services. All that steel, even the

antique landing pads, had to be purchased somewhere. Generators. Surveillance cameras. Drones. She pondered whether she could include a list of companies benefiting from the border-wall project in one of her articles. Would the e-zines she wrote for welcome that, or would it be too hot a subject to publicize?

Her fuel gauge read one quarter, so rather than risk running dry in the middle of the desert, she continued north toward the highway instead of backtracking south toward the wall.

Pulling down the visor to block a bit of the brutal sun, she mused that if she took that office job, she'd have plenty of time down here to follow jaguars and question the locals. Sliding the cover back on the visor mirror, she regarded her reflection. Her hair stood out in sweaty wisps, and her face was blotchy from the heat.

"Are you insane?" she chided herself aloud. "Besides, now you are probably persona non grata." She slid the cover back over the mirror. "Not to mention that you have never done any sort of accounting."

RTK was apparently another dead end. Trying to think of it instead as another potential lead she could now strike from her list, narrowing the possibilities, Sam made an effort to loosen her grip on the steering wheel.

A pronghorn abruptly materialized in the road, and she slammed on the brakes. Two more bounced onto the gravel and then over the ditch on the other side, vanishing into the brush. She remembered Maya saying she'd always wanted to see one of the antelopes, which really weren't antelopes at all, but the only living species of their kind.

Maya would probably call or at least send email again tonight, asking about her new-found half sister. Sam pounded the steering wheel. "Goddamn it, Jade, where are you?"

* * * * *

At dinner that evening, Sam looked for Diego Xintal, but didn't see him, so she sat with two couples wearing Broads name tags. Men, she had learned, were also part of the group, even if a minority. The group called them Bros.

At first, the chatter at their table was about one of the Broads, Linda, sighting a rare woodpecker, but then a Bro said, "I hear they found a headless body in a car lot in Nogales." His name tag identified him as John from Colorado Springs.

A cold shiver ran down Sam's spine.

"I've heard that's what happens if you cross the cartel," the other man, Tom, said.

With some trepidation, Sam asked, "Do they know who the victim was?"

"The news only said it was a Jeep salesman," John said. "He probably refused to donate a Jeep for transport, or maybe he said something to authorities."

Salesman. Not Jade, then.

"The guy's girlfriend is missing, too."

"Wonder what they do with the heads?" John's wife, Ardell, mused.

Sam felt nauseous. Silence reigned for a few long minutes as they all stared at their cherry crisp and considered the possibilities.

Finally, Linda piped up again in a cheery tone. "I've heard there are peccaries here. Or maybe you know them as javelinas. Have any of you seen one?" And the conversation switched back to happier topics.

When she was back in the dorm room, Sam found three email messages from Maya. The first tugged at her heart: Could you help me make a quilt square for sisters?

Sam had long been cross-stitching squares for a quilt that would represent her life. Her mother and grandmother had sewn the first squares. After their deaths, Sam had created her own designs to preserve her best memories. Not long after they'd met, Maya had asked Sam to show her how to cross-stitch. So far Maya had only two squares for memories that made her proud: one that represented her work on the trail crew, and one, a stack of books, that memorialized starting college.

The next two messages were the same: Where's Jade? She's not answering.

Taking a deep breath, Sam replied, Yes on the quilt block. Jade's still in the field. Unexpected delays.

To her surprise, a message arrived only a second later. I want to come join Jade. I can get some days off work and school.

A horrific vision of Maya's headless body flooded Sam's imagination.

Not possible, she wrote back, I don't know exactly where Jade is. At least that much was true. Be patient, I'll let you know as soon as she's back.

There were also multiple messages from the magazines to whom she'd promised articles. And her name was on the work schedule for tomorrow, both for breakfast and for dinner. She needed to stay here and work. It would be a relief to get back to her original plan for volunteering at the station.

Guilt rode in on the coattails of that thought, but Sam tried to force it out of her head. She still had no evidence that Jade was in trouble. Her roommate was simply missing, and Katrina had indicated that her daughter had vanished in the past, for days at a time. Jade kept camping supplies in her car. Still, Sam couldn't get rid of the nagging feeling that something wasn't right. For a Latina like Jade, the border area might be a more dangerous place than even Zimbabwe.

While rummaging for a clean washcloth among her roommate's belongings, Sam picked up Jade's small jewelry bag. Inside was a pair of silver-and-turquoise bird earrings, and another pair of braided copper and silver wire hoops. If Jade had possessed earrings like the one Sam had in her pocket, her roommate was wearing them now. Or she was wearing at least one. That was a disturbing thought.

Sam wished for a cat to pet right now; Simon's soft fur and accompanying purr would go a long way to soothe her jangled nerves. In the last three days, she'd put hundreds of miles on her SUV and talked to dozens of people, but she was getting nowhere. She hadn't found Jade or her car. She couldn't even find that jaguar's trail. And there was still the possibility that Jade was with Landon Imhoff, wherever he was.

One thing at a time. She couldn't face querying more people tomorrow. Hoping Diego Xintal was still in the area, she sent him an email message: I want to show you Jade's jaguar photo. I need your help.

# 11

To Sam's surprise, Diego Xintal was waiting for her in the dining room entryway when she reported at 6:30 a.m. for her volunteer shift.

"Got your message," he said. "Where's the photo?"

"Sam?" Bev called from the kitchen.

"Coming!" To Xintal, she said, "The photo's in my room. Do you think you can help me find that jaguar?"

"I don't know until I see the photo."

She checked her watch. "Can you wait for ninety minutes?"

"Sam! This fruit's not gonna chop itself!"

Xintal's expression was amused. "You better go before Bev runs in here with a knife. Catch me down by the hummingbird feeders when you're done."

Bev kept Sam so busy in the kitchen during breakfast and washing dishes afterward that she didn't have an opportunity to overhear any more talk among the Broads or researchers. As soon as she was able to hang up her dishrag, she trotted to her room and pocketed her cell phone.

Xintal was not sitting on any of the benches around the hummingbird feeders, but she spotted him close by, reclining in one of the rickety chairs around the moss-flanked retaining pond of creek water that also served as a swimming pool.

Pulling up a chair beside him, she handed him her phone. He studied the image of the jaguar for several minutes. Using his fingers, he enlarged the image and slid it around on the screen. A slight frown creased his forehead, but his expression was largely unreadable.

"This is El Guapo; I can tell by his spots. I can't believe he went down to the wall, and east of Naco, too." Xintal made a clucking noise with his tongue. "So dangerous." Meeting Sam's eyes, he said, "Only two jaguars have been spotted in the last decade in Arizona. Both were male. And someone showed up last year with the skin of the other, El Jefe."

"I read that. He was shot?"

Xintal glanced back at the phone, and his voice was sad as he said, "Or poisoned, maybe intentionally, or maybe he drank from one of the mine pits. They're death traps, you know."

"I know. People are scum."

Surprised by her comment, he only half stifled a laugh. "That's mostly true." Using his fingers on the phone screen, he enlarged the fence area. When he faced her again, Sam noticed that Xintal's eyes were a striking hazel, not the usual dark brown that was common with the black hair and bronze skin of most indigenous peoples of Mexico. "So as far as we know, El Guapo is the only jaguar left in Arizona. But I think I see why he would risk the trip to the wall."

She leaned close. "It's another jaguar, isn't it?"

"Looks like it might be."

"God." Sam leaned back in her chair.

"Nothing godly about this situation," he said.

"Can you help me track El Guapo?" she asked. "I found one paw print, but after that, I found a lot of marks that might be something. Then again, when it comes to jaguars, I don't know what I'm doing, especially in the desert."

"Jaguars are elusive, to say the least, and that's even more true of northern jaguars. Nobody knows much about them."

"If we can follow El Guapo, we might find Jade."

"We could find him sooner if we use dogs. I have a friend whose hounds are trained to track big cats."

She knew that hunters used dogs to track cougars, and that they'd likely track jaguars, too. But she didn't want to imagine what happened when the dogs cornered a jaguar. She'd read that jaguars could bite through the skulls of many animals. And packs of dogs were never benign, either. "I'd rather not."

Xintal continued to stare at the image on her phone until it went into sleep mode, blanking out the screen. He handed back the phone. "Okay, we'll do it your way, but no promises. Can you find that one paw print again?"

She nodded. "I marked the location."

"Can you leave tomorrow before dawn? Four thirty a.m.? And can you drive? My car is a piece of shit. Plus, if I'm driving, we're a lot more likely to get hassled."

Just thinking about getting up in the dark inspired an urge to yawn. Stifling the feeling, Sam said, "I'll make it happen."

"Hiking boots, food, and plenty of water. And camping gear, if you've got it. We might be out overnight."

"I camped my way across the country to get here."

"Perfect. Meet you at the visitor center." He held up a fist.

She bumped his fist with her own. "Deal."

Gaining an ally gave Sam new incentive. She finished her first article on the Sky Islands and sent it off to the magazine editors with a few photos, a suggestion that they add a map, a promise that the next article would feature the rare species that lived here, and that the one after would highlight the migration patterns of wildlife between the US "islands" and the Mexican ones. She'd make sure the wall was prominent in that last article, so readers could learn how the barrier would cut off the natural routes of many animals to find food, water, and mates.

After a brief walk on the trails around the station's grounds to clear her head and to search for the rare frogs that inhabited the local wetlands, she reported for dinner duty. As she walked among the tables collecting dishes to wash, the talk in one group was centered on a huge drug stash, mostly methamphetamines, found in a desert canyon forty miles north of the border. Another table was discussing migrants found dead of dehydration on the Tohono O'odham Nation Reservation to the west.

She overheard, "It was a mother and two little kids."

How sad. She lingered longest at the table where the Broads were discussing butterflies they'd seen that afternoon, identifying them with photos in an online app.

"There was a Mormon Metalmark."

"Elada Checkerspot."

"Two-tailed Swallowtail."

"Powdered Skipper. I saw three of them!"

Their enthusiasm was a good reminder that beauty still survived in this part of the world.

Back in her room, Sam used her internet-to-phone app to call her housemate Blake. She hadn't scheduled the call, but felt a need to connect with her peaceful world back in Washington State. The phone rang on his end so many times that she was about to tap End Call when he finally answered. "*Agh*! Shit! Goddamnit!"

"Blake?"

"*Agh!* I stubbed my toe on the bed leg. Ow, ow, ow!"

"Life is painful when you're a klutz."

"Did you call just to harass me, Sam?"

"More or less," she admitted. "I needed to hear some normalcy from the northwest corner of the country. Everything down here is heat and dust and spiky things, and drug smugglers and people dying in the desert."

"*Everything?*" he asked. "I thought you went there on purpose."

"Okay, not everything." This was exactly why she'd called Blake. He never let her get away with any crap. "There are incredible birds, especially hummingbirds, and butterflies and pronghorn antelope. Which really aren't antelope, by the way."

"I promise to call them pronghorn non-antelopes from now on. Although I can't really remember ever calling them at all before."

She laughed.

"But all the people in Arizona are dying or smuggling drugs? That must make for some strange conversations."

"It can, for sure. But there are some pretty cool folks here, too. Researchers and Great Old Broads."

"If I said that, you'd slap me."

"That's the name of the organization. Great Old Broads for Wilderness. There's a whole contingent of them staying here at the research station right now. And they're not all women."

"Male broads? Cross-dressers or trans?"

"I can't vouch for what they do in the privacy of their own homes, but here they all act like normal men, at least as far as I can tell."

"We're all *normal*, Sam." Blake's voice held a touch of acid now.

At times, talking to her gay housemate was like walking a tightrope. "You know I meant straight, Blake."

"Ah, but you left yourself open for that one; I just couldn't resist. Do I detect a hint that all is not wonderful down there?"

"I have a roommate here, or rather, I'm supposed to have a roommate, but now she's missing."

Blake's voice rose an octave higher as he yelped, "Jade is missing?"

"Wait!" Sam yelped in response. "How do you know her name?"

"What do you mean, *missing*?"

"Blake!" Sam abruptly realized that she was shouting, and lowered her voice before the volunteers in the room next door started banging on the wall. "Shut up and listen! Please tell me Maya's not there."

"Maya's not here."

"Good."

"But she told me all about her newfound sister, the famous wildlife photographer. And now you're telling me Jade Silva is missing?"

"Nobody's seen her for days. But she might just be out tracking a jaguar."

"Just?"

She ignored that. "I'm heading out tomorrow with a jaguar expert to find that same cat."

"Of course you are."

"Maybe I'll find Jade at the same time. Do not, I repeat, *not*, tell Maya that Jade is missing. I probably shouldn't have told you, but I thought you weren't involved, and I wanted to hear a sympathetic voice."

"This is more like a hysterical voice. And Maya will be here tomorrow. She wants me to show her how to change the tube in her bike tire."

"Find a way to tamp down your hysteria, Blake. I don't want to alarm Maya needlessly. How's my cat?"

"In the last almost-three weeks, Simon has brought me five mice and two shrews."

She chuckled. "He's trying to impress you."

"This morning he brought in a baby possum. I spilled my

coffee when that thing poked its snout out from under the couch."

"That *is* impressive. He's never brought me a possum. Was the poor thing okay?"

"No blood or anything. Apparently, playing dead just gets you kidnapped, not eaten. I guess Simon wanted a pet of his own. Anyhow, Claude wrapped up the victim in a towel, and we took it back to the woods."

"Thank Claude for me." Sam was glad to hear that Blake's relationship with his Canadian friend was apparently ongoing. "That sounds like more fun than playing with scorpions and rattlesnakes here."

"I'm sure that depends on your point of view."

"Okay, Blake, I'm going to wrap this up now. I just wanted to check in because I'll probably be out of cell range for a couple of days. I probably should call Chase, too. Thanks for cheering me up."

"Happy jaguar-hunting. Don't get eaten."

"Not a word to Maya, remember."

"I'll save you a mouse. Or three. There will be a whole herd of them romping around the house by the time you come back."

"Pet Simon for me. Bye, Blake."

Chase was not nearly as lighthearted and entertaining as her housemate had been. His tone was concerned as he echoed, "You're hunting a *jaguar*?"

"That's what I just said, Chase. With Diego Xintal. He's an expert. He's connected with a jaguar sanctuary in Mexico."

"How do you spell that?"

"J-a-g-u-a-r," she told him.

The silence on his end was deafening.

She sighed. "There's no need to run a background check on Xintal, Chase."

"S-h-i-?"

"It starts with an *X*. Diego's a good guy. I can tell. And Jade trusted him."

"And what happened to *her*?" he reminded Sam. "There's a border patrol agent missing, and a car salesman just got beheaded and five more migrants have died in the desert in the last two days."

"Five? I only heard about three. And I shouldn't have told you about the border patrol agent, so keep that to yourself; it's not public knowledge."

"I'm not the public, remember? Don't do it, Summer. You don't need to go out there. Leave this for the authorities."

"The authorities are too busy chasing border crossers and drug smugglers to care about one maybe-missing woman. And the jaguar is the only clue I can think of to follow right now. I just wanted you to know that I might be incommunicado for a couple of days. Maybe we'll find Jade, or at least some more clues out there, along with the jaguar."

"I'm afraid of everything you might find 'out there,' *querida*. That jaguar is the least of my worries. You could vanish just like Jade did."

She knew Chase was thinking about his horrific experience as an undercover agent in the Arizona desert. "This is different, Chase. I have a lot of experience in the wilderness, you know. And so does Diego. I'm not hanging out with wacko militia types planning to ambush migrants."

"It's the desert, not the North Cascades. And militia types and migrants and drug runners might ambush *you*. Can't you wait a few days? Nicole and I have to fly to Las Vegas tomorrow to chase down a couple of leads on this money laundering case. Then I'll fly to Tucson. You can meet me there, and we'll put our heads together and come up with a reasonable plan."

She watched a small blot move out from the shadows under her bed. Hard black outer wings marked it as a beetle, not a scorpion. "I'll think about that."

He made a guttural sound in his throat, then said, "Good luck finding the jaguar."

"Have fun with Nicole in Vegas." She thought her words sounded at least as sincere as his.

Another blot, this one a pale brown shape, scuttled after the beetle. A bona fide scorpion, this time, one of the tiny blond natives. She moved her feet up onto her bed.

"I love you, Summer."

"I love you too, Chase."

Grabbing her empty water glass, she ripped a piece of paper from her notebook, scooped both beetle and scorpion into the glass, slipped on her flip-flops, then walked outside into the darkness.

After strolling a few yards into the trees, she shook her captives out onto the ground. "Stay outside," she told them.

Stepping back, she paused to listen for night sounds before returning to her room. Goosebumps soon rose on her bare arms. At more than a mile in elevation from the desert floor, nights at the station were still cold in May. Tomorrow, she would find out what the weather was like at night down below, closer to the desert floor.

In her room, she checked her pack one last time to make sure she had everything she'd need for the next two days. Her RAV4 held four more gallons of water and her tent and sleeping bag. Before switching off her laptop, she took a last glance at Jade's jaguar photo.

Touching a finger to the screen, she whispered, "See you soon, I hope, Guapo."

# 12

They started the search not far from the wall, in the spot where Sam had found the stain and the paw print. As dawn crept over the horizon, she saw that the baking sun had almost completely erased the reddish color from the ground. So much for evidence.

"Yes." Xintal lightly touched a finger to the ground to the side of the print. "Most likely a jaguar."

"I was afraid it might be a puma. I expected a jaguar's paw to be larger."

"Jungle jaguars in Central and South America are bigger and heavier. Desert jaguars in the north are about the same size as mountain lions, usually no more than one hundred twenty pounds." Standing up again, he said, "Back to the car."

She gestured to the brushy hills ahead. "Aren't we—you—going to track?"

"It looks like he's headed toward the Pendregosas instead of the Huachucas. I know most of his favorite places. And he's several days ahead of us, so we'll start a few miles from here."

Sam grinned. She had guessed that Xintal knew far more about this particular jaguar than he had earlier let on.

As they neared the RTK compound, two groups of vehicles were exiting, one headed south toward the wall, and another smaller cluster, north. As a huge pickup passed, Sam noticed

Phil Thorensen in the driver's seat. When his gaze met hers, he stared for a few seconds, then raised a finger from the steering wheel in what passed for a wave in rural areas. The Straubs had certainly been right in reporting that the road traffic started at dawn in this area. There was no gear in the bed of Thorensen's truck. Maybe he was on the way to pick up materials, or maybe he was headed off to make another deal.

Sam spotted the dirt-colored van she'd seen before, but it had moved to a new location just off the road. Its dark windows seemed ominous. "Do you know what they're up to?" she asked her passenger, indicating the van with a tilt of her head as they passed.

"Don't know. Don't ask," Xintal responded.

Sam couldn't imagine anyone wanting to camp in this desolate area. She slowed. "They could be camping here. Maybe I should stop and ask if they've seen Jade."

Xintal put a hand on her knee. "Don't. I've seen that van several times. They're not camping."

If the van's owner was often in this area and up to no good, that seemed an even better reason to ask about Jade. She put her foot on the brake.

"Don't," Xintal reiterated.

Diego Xintal was familiar with dangers in the area; she wasn't. She swallowed, thinking about Jade, but pressed her foot to the accelerator and continued on.

Xintal's "few miles" turned out to be more like thirty by the time he had guided her to a narrow canyon that snaked up from the southwest into the mountains. According to the map, they were now less than twenty miles from the Southwestern Research Station. But that was twenty miles "as the crow flies," over the mountain peaks. In road time, it would take close to two hours to get there.

"Park there." Xintal indicated a small clearing with a

trailhead parking area a hundred yards past a sign marking the boundary of Coronado National Forest. If this sky island had been an island in the ocean, waves would be lapping at the shore right here. Instead, this altitude was the dividing line between different ecosystems, where the dry scrubby grasslands gave way to high mountains and forests.

Jumping out of the passenger seat, Xintal pulled his pack from the back of the RAV4. When Sam went to lash her small tent onto her pack, he said, "Leave the tent."

She looked at him, one eyebrow raised.

"We need to travel light and fast," he explained. "It's best not to sleep closed in, and we agreed to stay out just the one night. Take the sleeping bag, and if you must, take the rainfly so you can roll up in it if there's a thunderstorm. It's good to be able to keep a lookout all around."

That sounded ominous. But if Diego Xintal could make do with only a sleeping bag, so could she.

Traveling light wasn't easy with the need to carry multiple liters of water, and traveling fast proved difficult, too, as Xintal had much longer legs than she, not to mention that he was more acclimated to the heat. Even at seven thirty in the morning, to her the sun felt scorching at the low elevation. But each mile rose steeply in elevation, and the high walls of the surrounding mountains soon shadowed and cooled the valley by a few degrees.

They quickly departed from the hiking trail and wound their way through a forest of sycamores, oaks, and mesquite, constantly climbing. Xintal's gaze scoured their surroundings as they walked, and he stopped periodically to examine a scuff mark on the ground or a scratch on a tree. Most he judged as "old," shaking his head.

"How do you know these are jaguar signs?" Sam was amazed that he could decipher the subtle marks.

"From years of following them."

Finally, Xintal stopped at the base of a sycamore, where two broad scratch marks marred the white bark of the tree. Bending low, he sniffed. "Finally," he said, grinning. "He came by here not long ago. Maybe yesterday."

She knelt beside him. "I would have looked up higher for claw marks."

"These he made with his hind feet. And smell." Cupping his hand, he wafted the air from the mark toward Sam's face.

She bent closer, inhaled, then wrinkled her nose. "Musky."

"It would be stronger if it were today's. He's marking his territory."

Sam wondered what thoughts might go through a jaguar's brain when he encountered no scent from another jaguar. Would he be pleased that he had no competition? Or distressed that he was completely alone? Remembering Jade's photo of El Guapo at the wall, she decided that, at least at times, this jaguar was desperate to find a female of his species.

*Jade.* Sam had kept an eye out for the red CR-V along the roads, but had seen nothing. Plenty of human prints marked the bare dirt of the hiking trail, but she saw only vague rearrangements of the forest duff in the off-trail area she and Xintal explored. A damp spot near a spring held the cloven hoofprints of javelinas as well as a few tiny paw prints. Five toes and a pad, a print something like a house cat's. In a few of the tracks, there seemed to be an extra pad.

"Ringtail," Xintal informed her.

That explained it. She'd never studied ringtail tracks. "We have only raccoons where I live. I've only seen a ringtail once before, in Utah. I'd love to see one again."

"Maybe tonight."

Xintal was so focused she found it hard to keep up as he trotted from tree to tree and examined scuff marks on the ground. At one point, he admitted that he'd completely lost the jaguar's trail. "Might as well stop for lunch," he told her.

They parked themselves in the shade of a cliff to eat the snacks they'd packed. As she chewed the peanut butter sandwich she'd made, Sam heard faint voices in the distance. She rose to her feet, gazing in that direction.

"Leave it," Diego ordered in a quiet, firm voice, as if she were a dog. Then a second later, he murmured more kindly, "It's best to stay away from other people out here."

"But Jade—"

He shook his head. "It's not Jade. They're speaking Spanish."

She sat down again and listened more closely, recognized the cadence of a foreign language. A low voice that sounded urgent. Higher notes, like a woman or child. "Migrants?" she asked in a whisper.

He took another bite of the wrap he was eating. "Probably. I can't make out the words."

"Will they make it?"

"Depends on where they're going and who they are. The patrol monitors a lot of the established trails, so you never know."

The voices faded. Xintal took a last swallow from his water bottle and stood up. "Ready to move on?"

Summoning a second wind, Sam followed him along the base of an overhang. Xintal frequently glanced up at the side of the cliff as they walked, and she feared that he was looking for another, higher trail.

Dusk had already reached the valley through which they were traveling when she noticed an orange kerchief ground into the sandy soil near the base of a steep cliff. The kerchief was surrounded by a variety of boot prints. Stopping, they scanned the area, which was quickly growing dark.

A few feet off the ground, Sam spied a bundle wrapped in black plastic, stuffed into a crevice in the rock. Putting the toe of her boot into an indentation in the rock, she reached up for it.

Spotting the bundle at the same time, Xintal yelped, "Shit!" and grabbed her arm, jerking her down. "Don't touch it. Let's go."

"What the hell, Diego?"

"Let's go," he repeated in a low voice, his fingers still wrapped around her bicep. "This is none of our business. Let's go now." His gaze darted sideways before returning to her face.

A chill raced up her spine when she discerned a shadowy shape crouched in the shrubbery a few yards away. Then another, a little farther back. And maybe a third. The hairs on the back of her neck stood up.

"Yes, let's go," she echoed, rubbing her arm where he'd grabbed her.

*Drug runners?* She mouthed the word when they were a hundred yards from the package.

Nodding, Xintal whispered, "With guns," and continued to stride quickly up the canyon. She had to jog to keep up. What would have happened if she had pulled the package from the crevice? Or if they'd stayed longer? Had Jade, blithely following the jaguar, run into armed men? Was she lying somewhere close by? Sam wanted to zigzag and inspect the area more thoroughly, but Xintal's pace left her no option except to follow him.

They didn't speak again for at least a quarter mile. Sam was grateful she had a local guide. Left to herself, she would have pulled that package out of the cleft to investigate, in case it held a clue about Jade's whereabouts.

"Did that dirt-colored van belong to a coyote?" She pronounced the word the Spanish way so that he'd understand she meant a guide for undocumented migrants.

"Maybe," he responded. "Or it was an intermediate stop on the drug trail. It's best not to notice that sort of thing."

Sam kept thinking about how fearless Jade was. How she'd photographed armed poachers in Zimbabwe. How she was focused on wildlife. She might ignore dangerous humans out here, but would they ignore her?

"We need to go up," Xintal said. Finding a section that had finger- and toeholds, he climbed the mountain toward a rock bench set into the side of the cliff.

After Sam had heaved herself up after him, she found him once again bent over, this time examining abrasions on the rock. "Closer and closer."

She bent low to sniff. Yes, the jaguar's musk scent was stronger here. "Will we catch up to him before nightfall?"

"Doubtful," Xintal said, studying the darkening sky.

By the time the sun had set, they'd climbed over the ridge of a small mountain. At the top, they could see a road winding below. "We could have driven there," Sam noted mournfully.

"Not and followed El Guapo," Xintal reminded her. "We'll camp on that bench there." He pointed at a more level area a thousand feet down.

After studying the road below for any hint of a red CR-V, she followed him into the scrub brush down the mountain. The temperature rose as they descended, but the sun was setting and the night promised to be bearable.

Dinner was cheese and crackers and nuts and dried fruit. She checked her cell phone. No messages. No surprise—no signal here. In spite of what Xintal had said, Sam wished she had her tent to screen out the desert creepy-crawlies, rattlesnakes and scorpions and tarantulas. As she rolled out her sleeping bag, she even envisioned a Gila monster snuggling up to her during the night, but soon dismissed that. The fat, venomous red-and-black lizards were rare, after all. Just like that jaguar, she'd never seen one in the wild.

She was accustomed to the damp Pacific Northwest, where a camper was more likely to need protection against the rain, mosquitos, rodents, and the occasional bear. The celestial canopy overhead was far more interesting than the roof of her nylon tent, though.

"The stars here are stunning, Diego," she murmured softly, in case he'd already fallen asleep. "It's been too long since I've seen the Milky Way."

"They're planning to put floodlights all along the border wall," he responded. "And run generators to power them all night long."

Sam didn't want her imagination to go there, but of course it did, supplying a vision of endless miles of eighteen-foot-tall fence topped by looping concertina wire shining under blinding lights, as the hum of machinery drowned out all natural sounds. "I wish you hadn't told me that."

Xintal didn't reply.

She couldn't help thinking about the poor Straubs in their dream home, contending with not only the hideous, moaning wall and the traffic and dust but also with their nights lit up like a maximum-security prison.

A night bird cried in shrill, repeated notes. Sam tried to clear the unpleasant vision from her mind and take pleasure in the constellations above as she attempted to categorize the sound. Not a whistle, not a screech, not a hoot . . .

"Elf owl," Diego informed her. "It's close."

His words were proven by the barely audible sound of wings not far away. Sam wished she could see the tiny bird. An owl that could fit into a human hand! She hoped that little owl was eating its weight in scorpions this night.

She wanted a ringtail to come visiting. They were mostly nocturnal creatures. She wished away skunks, though, even the spotted ones down here. She'd had problems with skunks before, when camping in New Mexico.

A helicopter flew overhead, not too far away. Most likely the border patrol, probably equipped with infrared sensors to show body heat. Would she and Xintal show up on their screens? What would the agents make of two warm bodies lying on the ground in the national forest? The whop-whop of the rotors gradually faded away to the south.

The sound of that helicopter sparked a memory of an afternoon a week ago, when she was with Jade, taking pictures in Cave Creek Canyon. Sam had asked her roommate for photography tips.

"It's all about the angle and the light," Jade had said. "Take that butterfly, for instance." She'd pointed to a western tiger swallowtail sucking moisture from a damp spot along the trail, its wings slowly opening and folding. "If I take a photo of it now from directly overhead, my shadow will darken the image."

Sam understood that much. She said, "Sometimes that's more desirable when the sun's too bright."

"True. And sometimes you just need to wait for a cloud to move."

Patience, Sam mused. A virtue she'd never possessed. She needed to work on that.

"Now, if I take a photo from a three-quarter angle on this side, my shadow won't touch it, and that butterfly will have a distinct shadow of its own." Jade raised her camera to her eye and snapped a photo as the swallowtail unfolded its wings halfway.

"Angles and shadows can make or break a photo. I've shimmied up trees and climbed boulders to get the shot I want. But you've got to work with what's available. If I want a picture that's really different, I can try something like this. First, make sure to position yourself right." Taking a step to the side, Jade then quickly lowered her camera to the ground in front of the swallowtail and held the shutter button down, snapping several photos before the butterfly flitted away.

"You never know if one will come out, but it always pays to take a chance. Let's see what we've got." She picked up the camera and moved the last few photos into view. "The first," she said, holding out the camera so Sam could see.

It was a photo that most magazines would gladly accept, brilliant yellow-and-black-striped wings unfolding, the shadow on the ground echoing the scalloped edges of the butterfly's hindwings. "Nice," Sam said.

Pulling the camera back, Jade clicked the next photo into place. "And here's the next one."

Sam admired the head-on closeup of the swallowtail. Its spherical compound eyes were so huge, they made the butterfly's head look like a helmet. Two black antennae curved up and back in a *V* shape. Projections on the front of the swallowtail's head feathered around the top of its proboscis, which was elongated into a tube touching the damp earth between its outstretched front legs. The swallowtail's wings were spread, forming a brilliant-yellow backdrop for its head. Black stripes dripped like spilled ink down its forewings from the front edges.

"That's an amazing shot," Sam had told Jade. "You never realize how alien-looking insects are until you see them up close."

"It helps a lot when your subject stays in place." Jade had clicked to the last photo, then held the camera out again. "Last shot."

In that photo, the swallowtail had just lifted from the ground, caught in the process of curling its proboscis and legs, its wings raised halfway in flight. The live insect's similarity to a helicopter taking off was almost disturbing. *That,* Sam thought, *was the difference between mere picture taking and artistry.*

"I could stare at that image for hours," she'd told Jade.

"It's yours. I'll send all three to your email as soon as we have Wi-Fi again."

Jade was like that, generous. Patient. Persistent. She probably would have taken an incredible photo of that rattlesnake three days ago. If she were here now, Jade would probably be stalking that elf owl.

A grunt pierced the darkness, followed by another. Next, a low rumble filled the night. Sam lay tensely, feeling the reverberation as much as listening to the sound.

"That's El Guapo," Diego told her in a soft voice. "We're not far away. With luck, we'll catch up with our jaguar tomorrow."

And Jade, too, Sam hoped, even though today they'd found no signs of a human following the big cat. "Good night, Diego."

"*Buenas noches,* Sam."

To her surprise, she slept more soundly than she had since Jade had gone missing. But when she opened her eyes in the morning, the first thing she saw was the barrel of a gun aimed at her face.

# 13

"What you think you're doing here?" the man at the other end of the rifle barked.

"Uh," Sam stuttered, her heart seeming to beat as fast as a hummingbird's. "I *was* sleeping."

Three more men, one in a blue baseball cap and the other two in cowboy hats, stood not far away. The two in cowboy hats had their rifles trained on Xintal, who was fully dressed and sitting cross-legged on top of his sleeping bag. His hands were clasped together on top of his head.

"Are you American?" The man growled the question. He lowered the rifle stock from the tucked position against his shoulder, but kept the barrel pointed at her forehead. His eyes were hidden behind mirrored sunglasses. Graying blond hair straggled from beneath his red baseball cap, and his mustache was stained dark at its lower ends.

"Get your gun out of my face, please. We're both American." Determined not to show her fear, she rose up on an elbow, looking for the elastic that had bound her French braid last night. Ah, there it was, encircling her wrist. "We're backpacking."

"Huh," the guy huffed. "Hear that, Jimbo? They're *both* American, and they're *backpacking*."

"I'll just bet they are," the man in a sweat-stained gray

cowboy hat, maybe Jimbo, said. "Let's just see what sort of shit they're packing." Grabbing Sam's backpack, he unzipped it, spilling its contents into the dirt. The other cowboy, this one in a woven straw hat, had already dumped everything in Xintal's pack onto the ground.

Red Baseball Cap waved the rifle barrel in front of her face. "Get outa there. Slow-like."

Unzipping her sleeping bag, Sam rolled out, glad she was wearing her shorts and T-shirt, and hoping the gunman didn't notice that she was trembling. Forcing bravado into her voice, she asked, "Who are *you*?"

He lowered the barrel of his rifle a few inches. "We're the guys who protect this country from the likes of you. We're the Patriot Posse."

"Militia?" she guessed. She'd run into paramilitary types before on the Olympic Peninsula of Washington State.

"A well-regulated militia is necessary to the security of a free state," Red Baseball Hat retorted, then spat a stream of tobacco juice onto the ground.

Sam recognized the first part of the Second Amendment to the Constitution. Most NRA types knew only the second half about the "right of people to keep and bear arms."

"Exactly how is your miniscule militia of four regulated?" she asked.

Red Baseball Cap's mustache twitched. His jaw tensed. "Shut up!" Scuffing the dirt under his cowboy boots, he kicked gravel onto her sleeping bag. "We ask the questions here."

In addition to the rifle that each carried, all the intruders wore pistols in leather holsters strapped to their hips and tied to their thighs, like gunslingers from the Old West. The Patriot Posse members weren't well regulated, but they were certainly well armed.

"You're not law enforcement," Sam bluntly stated. "We're

on national forest service land. It belongs to all American citizens. We have as much right to be here as you do."

"You have no authority here," Xintal agreed.

"Zero authority," Sam echoed, pulling the elastic from her wrist. Could she use it like a slingshot and zing a piece of gravel into this bozo's eye?

Red Baseball Cap trained his rifle barrel on her again. "I said, shut up!"

The other three men pointed their rifles at Xintal. "You too. Shut up, Mex! *Cállate!*"

While three of the men were middle-aged and unkempt, with paunches hanging over their belts, the fellow in the blue baseball cap was young, with a stylishly trimmed beard and pale-blue eyes. He scared Sam most of all, because he seemed jittery, just waiting to jump into action.

The rifle barrel aimed between her eyes was making her cross-eyed. The shouting of the nutcase with his finger on the trigger was making her head ache. She heard Chase's voice in her head: *Summer, I worry that one of these days your smart mouth is going to get you killed.*

This might be the day he'd been fretting over. She knew that Jade, too, would be defiant if confronted by these yahoos.

"There's just, like, clothes and camping stuff in here." Using the toe of his cowboy boot, Straw Hat stirred her belongings, as well as Diego's, along the ground.

"Probably hid their stash somewhere close by." Red Baseball Cap scuffed more dirt onto her sleeping bag. "Why's a little bit of a gal like you helping this spic break our laws? You're aiding and abetting the enemy. That's treason."

When she didn't respond, he added, "You're a race traitor. That's what you are. Hey, guys, want to see if this little race traitor is a real blond? See if the rug matches the curtains?"

*Shit.* Sam clenched her teeth together to keep them from

chattering as she scraped her hair back into a ponytail. Why did women always have to worry about being raped before being murdered? Had Jade been raped and killed by these self-styled "soldiers"? Had they considered her fair game because she was Hispanic?

Straw Hat, spotting her wallet among the clothes and personal items in the dirt, picked it up. Opening it, he yanked out the cash and stuffed the bills into his back jeans pocket.

"Hey!" she yelped. "I saw that! Put my money back!"

"Never saw any money." Straw Hat dropped the wallet back into the dirt.

An ear-shattering boom made them all jump, and a bullet blasted a spray of dirt a few inches from Diego Xintal's right knee.

"Justin, what the fuck?" Straw Hat glared at the younger man in the blue baseball cap.

Gray Cowboy Hat blurted, "Shit!"

"That was an accident," Justin said, his eyes on the ground.

"The last thing we need is another 'accident' like last week," Red Baseball Cap said.

Justin retorted, "The Mex deserved it. You said so, too."

Sam's scalp prickled. Had this kid killed someone?

Justin refocused his glare and his rifle barrel on Xintal, snarling, "But now you know I'm not afraid to use it if I need to."

Sam's ears were still ringing a high-pitched whine, background noise to the wild thumping of her heart. These guys were loose cannons. What gave them the right to terrorize hikers on public property?

The terror that was vibrating through her body abruptly changed to rage. She'd had it with these self-righteous, self-appointed border guardians. Either they'd kill her or they wouldn't, but she didn't intend to die groveling.

"You're not patriots; you're common thugs. Diego is an American citizen, just like I am." She rose to her feet, her hands clenched in fists now. "You're the ones breaking the law, pointing guns in our faces. You better get the hell out of here before we press charges."

"I didn't say you could stand up. *Siéntase!*" Red Baseball Cap wildly waved his rifle barrel in the air, pointing it first at Sam's chest and then at her sleeping bag. "We're here to help the border patrol maintain security."

"Oh yeah? Let's see how grateful they are." She pointed behind him, where she was thankful to see two border patrol agents were making their way through the vegetation.

As the agents neared, she was surprised to recognize Alvarez and Bradley, who'd questioned her near the wall a few days ago. They hadn't seemed exactly friendly then. She had no idea what to expect from them now.

Stopping several yards away from the group, Bradley took a wide stance, planting his hands on his utility belt. "What have we here?"

Agent Alvarez copied his partner's military posture. The stance looked authoritative, imposing. Sam thought she might try that tactic sometime, although she doubted that it would appear as impressive when performed by a petite woman.

Xintal pushed himself to his feet. "We're backpacking in the national forest for a couple of days. Hiking. Camping. Birdwatching." He tilted his head toward his binoculars lying in the dirt with the rest of his possessions.

"And then these yahoos came along, and they're threatening us with rifles," Sam added. "And that one"—she pointed to Straw Hat—"just stole the money from my wallet."

Red Baseball Cap puffed out his chest. "Officers, we've determined that these two have no weapons, other than a pocketknife in her pack." He lifted his chin, indicating Sam. "They're not carrying much. So they probably hid their stash somewhere close by."

"Or they're waiting to join up with another group," Gray Cowboy Hat offered.

"They could be coyotes." This came from Blue Baseball Cap. "Probably headed down to the wall today to pick up a load."

Bradley scrutinized the group, his eyes narrowed. "We heard a gunshot."

"Just a warning shot, officer," Straw Hat said. "We needed to show these two we mean business."

"You four." After sliding his sunglasses down his nose with his index finger, Alvarez aimed a piercing gaze at each of the Patriot Posse thugs. "Clear out. This is your second warning. One more violation and we will slap handcuffs on all of you."

Sam wanted to ask why the Patriot Posse deserved three warnings. She doubted that most citizens who threatened someone with a gun received such consideration.

"The *ranchers* appreciate our help," Gray Cowboy Hat grumbled.

"Five minutes," Bradley warned, moving his right hand to the pistol holstered on his hip.

"Shee-it." Red Baseball Cap spat in the dirt, then walked away in the same direction that the border patrol agents had come from. The other three followed, swatting bushes with their rifles and kicking gravel along the way to show their displeasure.

"The guy in the straw cowboy hat stole money from my wallet," she repeated to the agents.

"Be glad that's all they took," Alvarez told her.

She told him, "I think that young guy, Justin, killed someone last week."

"I wouldn't be surprised," Bradley said. "You two shouldn't be out here. You know better, Xintal. You're leading our little Washington tourist astray."

Diego Xintal's head came up. "She's a wildlife biologist. I'm showing her the countryside. The national forest."

"Always gotta stir up trouble, don't you?" Alvarez shook his head. "You know that wandering around this area is not wise right now." To Sam, he added, "It's dangerous."

"Obviously," she said.

Bradley addressed her. "You could get shot. Might be on purpose. Might be by accident." His hand still rested on his pistol.

"And law enforcement is not going to help if we get into trouble." Sam tried to stare Bradley down, but his eyes were still hidden behind mirrored sunglasses.

Alvarez either cleared his throat or growled at her.

"You guys cover a big territory," she observed. "I'm surprised to see you here."

"Expanded duty," Bradley commented. "We're an agent short right now."

He had to be talking about Landon Imhoff.

"I'm still searching for my friend, Jade Silva," Sam told them. "Want to see her photo again?"

"Be on your way," Bradley snarled. "Both of you." The agents turned to leave.

Sam asked their departing backs, "Have you found Agent Imhoff?"

Both agents did an about-face. Snagging his sunglasses with a finger to slide them down his nose just as his partner had previously done, Bradley examined her with intense blue eyes. "What do you know about Agent Imhoff?"

Sam abruptly remembered that the patrol agent's disappearance had not been announced to the media. That information had come from Nicole's cousin, Maria. "I'm a friend of Naomi's," she lied. "You know, Landon's fiancée."

Narrowing his eyes, Bradley studied her for a long, awkward moment, then shifted his piercing gaze to Xintal, whose face remained impassive. Then Bradley slid his sunglasses back into place, obscuring his eyes again.

"Clear out," he told them. He strode off in the direction from which he'd come.

Before Alvarez followed his partner, he said, "Have a nice day." Apparently, he was always the closing act for the twosome.

Diego Xintal, muttering in Spanish, loaded his backpack with his scattered belongings, shaking the dirt from his sleeping bag.

"What the hell was all that about?" Sam asked.

He groaned. "That was a visit from the Arizona Borderland Welcome Wagon."

"Agent Bradley knows you?"

"And you, too, apparently." Xintal stuffed the last of his clothing into his pack and zipped it up. Slinging his binoculars around his neck, he flapped a hand toward her. "Hurry up. Let's go find El Guapo."

"And Jade."

"You can hope." He smoothed his long hair back from his face, tucking it more tightly into the elastic band that captured his ponytail. "But so far, I've seen nothing to indicate that Jade was tracking the jaguar. And as for El Guapo, let me remind you that it will be a miracle if we actually see him. Jaguars are experts at invisibility."

"So I've heard." She laced up her hiking boots. "I promised Bev I'd be back tonight."

"And I promised my wife. All the more reason to hustle." He pointed toward the mountain crest. In the sky beyond, a pair of immature golden eagles were circling on the rising thermals.

A blue-throated hummingbird magically materialized and danced for a few seconds in front of Sam's face, flashing its brilliant feathers. Then it zipped away. "Did you see that?" she asked.

"Good omen," Xintal commented.

After buckling on their packs, they strode upward. Sam chewed a granola bar as she walked, washing it down with swallows of lukewarm water.

Two more hummingbirds buzzed them as they hiked. It was hard to focus on the jewel-like birds as they darted about, but she thought they were rufous males.

More birds chattered in the trees around them. When Sam spied a cavity in a sycamore branch, she stopped to study it. Sure enough, a pair of tiny owlets filled it, their feathers still downy, their dark eyes squeezed shut. Maybe they were sleeping; maybe they believed no predator could find them if they couldn't see it. The angle was crap, but she snapped a photo anyway, then held up the phone and took another picture on high, hoping she was aiming the camera at the right spot. She checked the result. The nest wasn't centered, but she could crop the image in Photoshop.

Scanning the higher branches for the owl parents, Sam noticed an unusual pattern among the leaves. Raising a hand, she shielded her eyes against the glare of the rising sun.

And there he was. El Guapo.

She'd never seen a more majestic creature.

His green-gold gaze burned intensely into hers. The hairs on the back of her neck stood up as she abruptly recalled reading that the name "jaguar" was derived from a native term meaning "'he who kills with one leap."

But this jaguar seemed relaxed at the moment. Sam could

soon make out his legs as he stretched the length of a branch. His face was striking, with beautiful golden fur flowing from the crown of his broad head into the ivory of his muzzle, where white whiskers sprouted from rows of black spots. Ebony markings like heavy eyeliner encircled his burning amber eyes; splashes of black ink freckled his broad forehead and cheeks. Sam knew that the markings of each jaguar were unique. El Guapo had three short vertical stripes above each eye, like a row of apostrophes.

Xintal stood beside her, barely breathing. "*Hola, amigo,*" he whispered. "I'm glad to find you healthy."

The jaguar did look healthy, at least what she could see of his body among the leaves.

Both Sam and Xintal admired the big cat for several minutes in silent awe. But when Sam raised her phone to take a photo, El Guapo apparently decided he'd had enough of the paparazzi. He spat, stood up on his limb, then hissed at them. Remembering Jade's lecture on taking chances, Sam kept her aim on the jaguar and her finger on the shutter button as she and Xintal shifted in different directions, moving back from the sycamore. Walking backward, she nearly tripped, barely managing to keep the lens pointed in the right direction as El Guapo leaped to the ground. He swept his royal gaze over them, gave one last growling cough of warning, then loped into the forest.

"Wow," Sam gasped, just then realizing she'd been holding her breath.

"Yeah, wow," Xintal echoed.

"I understand why natives worshipped them. Heck, I'm worshipping jaguars from here on out," she told him.

He grinned. "I've worshipped them for years."

"I met a jaguar," she said in wonder. Then, coming down a little from the euphoria, she added, "But no sign of Jade."

Xintal started to hike down toward the road below.

"Wait, Diego!" Sam yelped. "That's where we came from." She pointed back over her shoulder, indicating the crest of the mountain and beyond.

"Hitting the road down there and walking around is safer," he told her.

Drug smugglers, migrants, vigilantes in the woods. "Good point."

They zigzagged down the hill toward the road. Sam studied the terrain as they descended, keeping an eye out for a tent or a pack or the glint of a camera lens, or even a print that could have come from Jade's boot. She saw only Xintal's prints ahead of her.

Another dead end. If Jade had started out following the jaguar, she'd stopped long ago. But where and when? Sam cursed herself for being so naive as to believe it would be possible to locate her roommate out here. Jade could have hidden in thousands of places, even within the relatively small area they'd traveled through in the last two days. Jade could have vanished somewhere, anywhere, with Agent Imhoff. This was an impossible quest for one lone woman to take on.

Sam was bitterly disappointed about not finding Jade. This was the seventh day her roommate was missing. She had no idea how Xintal felt; the man was stoic, but he'd only known Jade as a famous wildlife photographer, not as a friend.

However, they were both exultant about seeing El Guapo. "Do you know how rare it is to see a jaguar up close like that?" he kept asking her. "Especially without using dogs to find him."

"It was a magical moment I'll never forget," she told him truthfully. "I could never have found him myself."

Diego was right, descending to the road and then walking around to their parking spot saved them several hours of hiking back the way they'd come. As Sam drove out of the mountains, her cell phone pinged, signaling that it had coverage again. Then there were several more pings, indicating incoming email or text messages.

"Can you read them to me?" she asked Xintal.

He laughed at the first one. "From Bev: Desperate for help tonight. Not going to desert me, too, are you?"

"Tell her we're on our way back. ETA seventy minutes."

He thumbed the response into her phone for a few seconds, then told Sam, "There's a message from Starchaser. Subject says: 'Staying out of trouble?'"

Chase. "Don't read that one; it's personal."

"Okay. This last one is from someone named Maya. No message, but the subject says 'Where are you? Where is Jade?'" He returned the phone back to the cupholder where she'd placed it. "So, this Maya is also looking for Jade? Is she a relative or a friend?"

"That's a long story." Sam pressed her lips together. She was still no closer to answering Maya's question, and sadness felt like a lead weight in her chest. Frustration was literally weighing her down.

She'd seen a jaguar in the wild, she reminded herself. And she had photos of her own to prove it.

# 14

Sam barely had time to shower before she was sucked into dinner duty, chopping and serving and washing. It was the last night of the Great Old Broads gathering, so there was no lecture this evening. That was just as well, because she didn't think she could keep her eyes open during a talk.

Her dorm room had grown hot during the day, and she opened the window to let in the cool evening breeze. She was downloading her jaguar photo from her phone to her computer when a knock sounded at her door. Then it opened. When Holly peeked in, Sam was glad she was still fully dressed. "Hey, there's a call waiting for you on the landline in the dining hall. Good thing I heard it ringing when I was restocking supplies. The woman asked for Summer Westin, but that's you, isn't it?"

"That's me." As she strolled through the growing darkness to the other building, Sam's anxiety rose into her throat. If someone was calling her on the station landline, it had to be an emergency, didn't it? Chase, Maya, and Blake knew to use the internet to connect with her. Was a law enforcement official calling to tell her that one of them had been injured or killed? She couldn't bear that thought. She'd lost two dear friends to murder just last year, and others to accidents before that. When she'd volunteered here, she'd never imagined her stay might be dangerous.

Maybe it was a ranger from the Coronado Forest Service office; she remembered now that they would know to call the Southwestern Research Station if they couldn't reach her cell phone. It didn't have to be bad news, but Jade had been missing so long, it was hard to stay hopeful.

Bracing herself, she picked up the phone. "This is Summer Westin."

It was indeed a law enforcement official, but not one from Washington State. Deputy Ortega sounded apologetic as she said, "The CR-V of that friend you were trying to find, Jade Silva, has been located. I thought you might want to know."

"Where?" Sam asked. Then, belatedly realizing that Ortega was doing her a favor, added, "Thank you."

"In an arroyo not too far from Tombstone. Some people use those creek beds as roads during the dry season. The CR-V was well off the highway, hidden among some trees. Looks as if some migrants may have been sleeping in it, but overall it's in pretty good shape with only a small dent in the back bumper."

That didn't make much sense to Sam, but at this point little else did, either. Why would Jade have driven there? "Was there camping equipment in the back? Camera gear?"

"No. If there were valuables left inside, they were probably stolen days ago. We didn't find any sign of your friend. There were, however, traces of blood in the cargo area of the vehicle."

Blood. *Oh God.* The jaguar had looked fine, so . . . "Is it human blood? Will you send it for testing?"

"We already know it's human blood. But we don't know if it's hers. She might have picked up an injured migrant or have hurt herself somehow."

"Will you send it for DNA testing, or blood typing, or whatever it is that you do?"

"We have nothing to match it to."

Sam did a quick mental inventory of the belongings her

roommate had left in the dorm. Jade's hairbrush still remained in her desk drawer, and her toothbrush was no doubt still there, too. And Sam remembered a sweat-stained baseball cap that still dangled from a hook on the wall. She listed all those items for Ortega.

"There are no guarantees, but if you bring them all in, we might be able to extract DNA from one of them."

"I'll bring them to the sheriff's office. Can you list her as officially missing now?"

"We've towed the car to our impound lot. If nobody calls about it, I guess we can assume she didn't abandon it voluntarily."

*About damn time*, Sam thought.

"But as I previously mentioned, adults—"

"Have a right to go missing," Sam finished for her. "But she walked away from a volunteer job, and she hasn't communicated with anyone for a week now. And she wouldn't abandon her car like that."

"We'll put her on our missing list. But all that means is that local law enforcement will receive her driver's license photo and description. Don't expect a manhunt or anything like that. We still have no evidence that a crime, other than perhaps a car theft, has occurred. And you should know that without an arrest or a court case pending, DNA testing will take weeks or even months. The system is overloaded."

Sam contemplated throwing the receiver across the room in frustration. Fortunately, it was attached to the base by an old-fashioned cord. She took a deep breath. "Thank you, Deputy Ortega. I'll bring those items I mentioned to you tomorrow."

She needed to call Jade's mother, but she didn't have her number with her. As she trudged back to her room in the dark to retrieve it, she tried to imagine what she was going to tell

Katerina Franco. Your daughter's still missing, but they've found her car. And there's blood in it. Would Katerina continue to believe that Jade was just on walkabout somewhere?

The location of the CR-V made it unlikely that Jade had taken off with Imhoff, because his border patrol SUV had been found nearly fifty miles away in Douglas. Sam couldn't see how the two missing people were connected. Maybe Imhoff had decided to simply walk away from his job and his pregnant fiancée. Poor Naomi.

But Jade? Why would she have driven from the wall north toward Tombstone? Maybe she'd been carjacked. A prickle ran down Sam's back as she remembered the plastic-wrapped package, the shadowy figures hiding in the bushes along the trail yesterday. Sooner or later, drug smugglers would need a vehicle, wouldn't they? Or maybe they needed a new vehicle, a vehicle unknown to the border patrol, she thought, remembering the dirt-colored van she'd spotted twice in the area.

As she retrieved Katerina's phone number from the dorm room, Sam's brain conjured up a horrific vision of Jade pistol-whipped and tossed into the back of her own CR-V by men in ski masks.

No. She needed to be more optimistic, for Katerina's sake. The blood could have another explanation. Jade could simply have needed to change a tire and cut herself on the jack somehow. Or as Deputy Ortega had suggested, she might have picked up an injured migrant. Jade would do that, Sam was sure.

But then what had happened? Shit, was she *any* closer to finding Jade? And why couldn't she light a fire under anyone else to help her? She trudged back to the dining hall and the landline phone.

Fortunately, she didn't have to explain any of her theories to Katerina, because the call went to voice mail. She left a message saying that Jade's car had been found, along with the phone number for the Cochise County Sheriff's Office.

Laughter wafted up the slope from the Broads meeting as she plodded back to the dorm. Checking her watch, she realized it was only eight thirty. She still had time to call Maya and Chase. But did she want to? Maya would panic, for sure. Chase would be sympathetic, but could he be helpful in any way? She didn't see how.

As her fingers touched her doorknob, Sam heard sounds from inside her room. Scuttling or rifling noises, as if someone were tossing the place. She'd had it with this "no locks" policy. Shoving the door open, she loudly complained, "What the hell is going on in here?"

The window screen had popped out and now lay on top of Jade's desk. Her jar of peanut butter had been tossed from the box in the closet corner, and several half-eaten pieces of bread were strewn across Jade's side of the room. Sam panicked, searching for her laptop, her thumb drives, her wallet hidden beneath her clothes. All there.

Had she been invaded by a hungry border crosser? She'd read of frantic migrants breaking into houses for food and water, but this had to be one desperate and none-too-bright character to climb five thousand four hundred feet in elevation to break in here.

Then she heard a scuffling sound under Jade's bed. Holding her breath, Sam bent down. With no weapon, the best response she could summon would be to run for the door.

Two bright eyes, ringed with ivory fur, warily regarded her above a long, pointed, upturned snout. The creature sat back, wrapped a thick tail about its hind legs, and raised a half-eaten slice of bread toward its mouth. It took Sam a moment of staring to realize that her food stash had been raided by a coatimundi. She'd read that the Chiricahuas were the northern boundary of their range, but she'd never before seen one in the wild.

Raccoons were frequent intruders near her home in Bellingham. They'd moved into the attic of Chase's old cabin and had fiercely fought for their squatters' rights there. The masked bandits were much cuter than this cousin, but she had no love for raccoons. A coati, on the other hand, was exotic. Especially one in her dorm room. Quickly grabbing her phone, she snapped a photo of the animal. The flash sent the intruder into a panic. Emitting complaints that were halfway between growls and clicks, the coati scuttled rapidly toward the open window. Now that it had emerged into the light, she saw that its tail was subtly banded with darker rings.

After the coati had exited, Sam pushed the window screen back into place and slid the pane to leave the window open only a crack.

Now she had another upbeat story to report to Chase and Maya in addition to her news of seeing the jaguar. She sent them both a photo of the coati. To Chase, she added the news about Jade's car. To Maya, she merely typed Jade is still out. I'll let you know as soon as I hear from her.

Opening Photoshop, she brought up her photo of El Guapo in the tree. It was a good image. She brightened the colors a bit and touched up the contrast and saved a copy. She'd use it tomorrow in an article about the jaguars that had been sighted in Arizona. One of El Guapo leaping to the ground was usable, too. The others were blurs.

After breakfast duty. And after she took Jade's hairbrush, toothbrush, and baseball cap to Deputy Ortega, she thought grimly. She'd better hit the sack if she was going to get up early enough to do all that. Shutting down her computer, she changed into her pajamas, slid into bed, and switched off her lamp.

"I found El Guapo, Jade," she told the empty bed. "He's fine. Well, as fine as a lonely jaguar can be. Please give me a clue about where you are. And please, please, please be okay."

It was hard to stop her imagination from speculating about the blood in Jade's car. *Remember the fantastic things you've seen in the last two days*, she told herself. *Think of the hummingbirds, think of El Guapo, think of the coati. Think of the call of the elf owl, think of the owlets in their cavity nest.* But the voices of invisible migrants and the shadowy figures of evildoers and the menacing self-righteous mugs of the militia thugs kept intruding into the video playing out behind her eyelids.

She wanted to be back in her own bed, with a cat sharing her pillow on one side and Chase on the other. She wanted to taste Blake's latest culinary experiment and read a good book that would transport her somewhere wonderful. She even wanted to help Maya study for her biology final.

A great horned owl hooted outside. Nature's night song. It hooted again, then a third time. Tonight, there was no answer.

# 15

While chopping fruit for breakfast, Sam told Bev about the coati.

"Oh, yeah," Bev said. "She's been around awhile. Don't encourage her; she's a thief. You're lucky she didn't bring her whole mob."

"There's a mob?"

"Sometimes. Maybe just her kits."

"Does she have a name?"

"Some of the staff call her DC. Damn Coati."

"I'm thinking about calling her Jade."

Bev stopped stirring the coffee cake batter to give Sam a look. "Oh, hon. What's the latest on that girl?"

Sam told her about last night's phone call, about Jade's CR-V being found near Tombstone. "And there's blood in the cargo area. Human blood. But so far, no sign of Jade."

"Well, then, we've got to hope for the best, don't we?" Bev focused on the mixing bowl in her hands.

After breakfast, Sam chatted with Chase via the video app. He was at Sea-Tac airport, preparing to fly to Las Vegas with Nicole, and wearing a suit and tie. "I got your message last night, *querida*. I'm sorry the case has taken a downturn like that. But try to stay optimistic; there might be a simple explanation for everything."

"The Sheriff's Department still doesn't seem very interested. They told me DNA testing could take *months*. And I'm the only one who is actively searching for her."

"But you said that the deputy was adding Jade to the missing list."

"Apparently that only means they'll take note if they run across her."

Chase ran a hand through his dark hair. "I've heard law enforcement is overwhelmed right now down there. I'm so glad you'll be home in less than three weeks."

Sam had no intention of going back to Washington without knowing what had happened to Jade. She hoped that knowledge would come before she was scheduled to depart.

Out of sight, Nicole murmured something. Chase reached for the screen. "Sorry, gotta go, the plane's boarding. I'll call you from Las Vegas the first chance I get. Please don't go wandering around in the wild by yourself."

She didn't reply to that. She'd damn well go "wandering around in the wild" by herself whenever she felt like it. Chase should be used to that by now.

"I love you." He closed his laptop.

More frustrated than ever, Sam drove to Bisbee to surrender Jade's hairbrush, baseball cap, and toothbrush to the sheriff's department. She had to give the deputy at the desk Jade's name twice, which told Sam that Jade's case was such a low priority that word hadn't even gotten around the station. By the time she returned to the oven that was her SUV, her jaw ached from clenching her teeth so hard.

She went back to the little café she'd visited before, this time choosing vegetable soup and a cheese sandwich. As she'd hoped, the gray cat, Freddie, was there, lounging in the shade of a shrub in the little patio. She welcomed him onto her lap and sat stroking his fur. Blake had better be petting

Simon every day.

Law enforcement, even Chase, was not going to help, at least not in any timely manner. Jade could be anywhere. Kidnapped, injured, lying bleeding in a ditch, praying for someone to save her. Held captive by drug runners or human traffickers. All the public's focus was on the migrant problem and the crimes that some illegal border crossers perpetrated, often victimizing their own countrymen who were seeking a better, safer life. Sam needed to find some way of getting more attention from someone, anyone, to search for her roommate *now*.

This had all started with Jade's photo of El Guapo up against the border wall. It certainly wouldn't hurt to call attention to the jaguar photo and educate Americans about how the wall was severing natural migration routes, blocking wildlife from the food and water sources they needed, and barricading them from finding mates. That barrier might even make some species go extinct, or at least cause them to vanish forever from the United States.

Sam could think of only one person she knew who would be perfect for the job she had in mind. Before she'd met Chase, she'd been involved with Adam Steele, a handsome, up-and-coming television reporter. Years ago, he'd not only pushed her in front of the proverbial bus but also floored the accelerator and run over her by sensationalizing her online reports when cougars had been accused of snatching a child from a campground. Adam's role in inflaming public opinion had caused a friend to be shot, and nearly caused the deaths of dozens of innocent mountain lions.

When Sam couldn't forgive him for what he considered to be captivating news coverage, Adam had acted hurt. But he hadn't been so bruised by their breakup that he didn't promptly accept a promotion to a TV news anchor position at a California station.

She rarely heard from Adam these days, except when he called to complain that she should have shared whatever story she'd written about with him. Sam was well aware that telling Adam anything important was akin to handing the reporter a stick of dynamite and a book of matches and telling him to go play. Adam Steele had a tendency to dramatize every subtle hint to its most titillating possibility.

But he'd been the one to rescue her when she was a fugitive in the Galapagos Islands, so now it felt as though the scales between them were not quite balanced. She might have helped Adam launch his TV career, but she'd done that unwillingly, while he'd worked hard to galvanize the forces to evacuate her from Ecuador.

Sam had been involved with Chase at that time, but her FBI lover had been MIA, working undercover when she'd needed him. Chase was still not over the fact that he hadn't been her hero then.

And here she was, in a similar situation with Chase being his secretive FBI self in Las Vegas with Nicole when Sam desperately needed, or at least desperately wanted, his help.

She stared at her contact list for a long minute. Was that still Adam's personal number? Her watch told her it was just a little after 2:00 p.m. Adam was not on air until 6:00 p.m. in San Diego. Sucking in a breath, she tapped the call icon.

She was preparing her speech for his voice mail when to her surprise, Adam answered. "Babe! Are you in jail in a foreign country again?"

"Funny."

"That's the only time you ever call me."

She was glad he couldn't see her grimace. "I'm not in jail. I'm not even in trouble. As a matter of fact, I just ran across a story that you might be interested in."

"A local story? Are you in California? And if you are, why haven't you called me?"

"No. I'm not in California; I'm in Arizona. And I *am* calling you."

"So you are, babe. What's going on in Arizona that might interest me? Wait—this will have something to do with an animal, right?"

"Sort of."

"I knew it!"

"Do you want to hear this, or not? And stop calling me 'babe.'"

"Lay it on me. I hope it's something juicy that will make the national news feed. I'm tired of sticking to San Diego stories."

"I think this might do it." She told him about the photo, about Jade vanishing, about how she was having so much difficulty interesting anyone in the case.

"Is she pretty?" he asked.

That was annoying. "Yes, Jade is very attractive."

"Send me her photo."

Gritting her teeth, Sam sent it via text.

After a few seconds, Adam said, "Yes, this could work. Now, send me that photo of the jaguar at the wall."

"Jade entrusted me with it."

"If it's as good as you say, I can promise you at least a thousand for its use on TV."

"I'm not calling you because I'm looking for money."

"I get it, babe; we need to find your friend. But FYI, a thousand is peanuts to the network for an exclusive. And you can still use that photo in print however you want."

She'd hoped he'd say something like that. "Sending it now in a text."

There was a long pause, then he said, "Yeah, this could be

big. With the missing girl, this could be major! Everyone's talking about the wall, but all they've got is those miserable migrant detention facilities."

Sam fretted about Adam's use of the phrase "all they've got," like the inhuman conditions that migrants were held in weren't noteworthy because they'd already been highlighted on air. Some stories deserved to be pounded into the public's consciousness until the problems were resolved, didn't they?

"Where, exactly, are you?" Adam asked. "I can be there the day after tomorrow."

"Really?" She told him about the Southwestern Research Station.

"Can you book me a hotel room there?"

"Um . . . no hotels there. You'd be lucky if I can get you a room in the dorm. Maybe there's something in Portal. That's the closest town, or maybe I should say 'settlement.' It's very small."

"Line up everyone I need to talk to."

Uh-oh. She didn't feel comfortable telling Adam about Maria Gage or Deputy Ortega or even Jade's mother. "See, that's the problem. I haven't convinced much of anyone to talk to me."

A sigh permeated the airwaves. "Never mind, babe. You've forgotten how good I am. I'll shake some nuts off those Arizona trees."

Sam worried about what that might mean, but any action would be better than none. "I look forward to that, Adam. See you soon."

# 16

Sam spent the next day at the research station, doing double kitchen duty for breakfast and dinner. The job was much easier now that the Great Old Broads had vacated the premises. The sixty conservation advocates were replaced by the station's more typical guests: twenty-two new researchers. They were of all ages, mainly entomologists, herpetologists, and ornithologists. There was also one botanist, and a writer documenting the history of the research station for a book.

Sam got back to her own writing, working on articles for two conservation groups and taking photos of the area to accompany the text. As she strolled through the canyons in the afternoon, she continually examined the tree limbs overhead, hoping to catch a glimpse of El Guapo. A jaguar could easily travel the twenty-plus miles up and over the mountains from the place she'd last seen him. But after a while, it seemed crazy to continue searching the tree canopy for a big cat.

As she walked, she fretted about Jade's fate, about how long she could stall Maya, and about the havoc she may have unleashed by inviting Adam back into her world. After returning to her room, she added a watermark to her enhanced photo of the jaguar at the wall and included it in queries to several magazines. She wanted to write a feature article about how the border wall was disrupting migration routes, and

about how the construction, maintenance, and constant
patrolling of the barrier was already destroying local
environments. She mentioned the Earthship property as a
prime example of how a formerly pristine environment had
been changed, along with the lives of its inhabitants. She felt
certain that the Straubs would agree to be included if she
landed a deal to write an in-depth feature.

After her evening kitchen duty was finished, she returned
to her dorm room, and at 10:00 p.m., she decided to make an
early night of it. She had just slipped into her sleep shorts and
T-shirt when someone knocked on her door. She waited,
counting to ten. On seven, Holly opened the door and stuck
her head in. The housekeeper was beaming, and her voice was
higher than usual as she chirped, "You'll never guess who I
have here!"

Jade? Sam's heart leaped at the thought. Was everything
going to work out happily after all? No, that didn't make sense.
Jade would have simply walked in.

Holly opened the door wide and stood with her back
against it, admiring the tall, blond, drop-dead-gorgeous man
who passed in front of her, wheeling a small suitcase. Adam
turned briefly to flash a grin at the head housekeeper. "Thanks
so much, Holly. I'll take it from here." Grasping the edge of the
door, he gently pushed it shut, sweeping Holly back into the
night.

"Sammy!" He held out his arms.

"Adam." Sam stayed frozen in the position in which Holly
had surprised her, one knee on her bed, one hand pulling up
the blanket. "I thought you were coming tomorrow."

She hadn't taken a shower or even brushed her hair before
getting ready for bed. She planned to do all that in the morning
so she'd look her best long before the reporter arrived.

Adam let his arms drop back to his side. "It's your fault,

for turning me onto this exclusive. The sooner we start, the better, don't you think? I've only got four days to make a story out of this. I thought you'd be glad to see me."

"I am." She stood up and walked the few steps to him. Wrapping her arms around Adam in a brief hug, she said, "Thanks for coming," and then stepped back.

He wheeled his case forward. "Did you line up everyone I need to talk to?"

"I'll help all I can, Adam, starting first thing in the morning. But right now, I plan to sleep." Sam yawned.

Sitting on Jade's bed, he ran his fingers through his hair. "I could use some shut-eye myself. I've been hustling ever since you called yesterday, pulling everything together."

"Did you find a place to stay in Portal?"

"The crew did." Adam patted Jade's pillow. "This bunk's not taken, is it?" He swept his hands around his thighs, smoothing the blanket beneath him. "This is where she slept, right? Jade Silva, the missing girl." Surveying Jade's desk, he leaned over and picked up one of the small carvings there.

Sam felt a flush of irritation at his presumption. "I thought you only stayed in five-star hotels these days."

Setting the carving of the javelina back onto the desk, he patted Jade's pillow again. "I can slum."

Sam heaved a sigh. It was hard to believe they'd once been lovers.

Adam was not dense, though, and his expression changed to chagrined. "You know what I meant, Sam. You're not going to make me sleep in my rental car, are you? Or drive down the mountain in the dark to sleep on a cot in the same room with Alex and Dean."

She yawned again. "I suppose not. But you're staying in that bed, and I'm sleeping in this one."

"Excellent." After slinging his suitcase on top of Jade's

chair, Adam pulled off his jacket and began to unbutton his shirt.

"Before you peel down to your skivvies," she warned him, "You may want to consider that the shared bathroom is across the courtyard." She pointed in the general direction. "You can use Jade's towel."

"Retro," he commented. "It's like frat life all over again." After slinging Jade's blue towel over his shoulder, he extracted a leather dopp kit from his suitcase, then walked out, barefoot, closing the door behind him.

She should probably tell him about the scorpions.

Sliding her hairbrush from the drawer of her desk, Sam combed the tangles from her long blond hair. Then she switched on the reading lamp over Jade's bed, now Adam's, and climbed back into her bed and switched her lamp off.

"Did you see that guy?" a female voice outside her door asked. Sam thought the speaker was one of the new researchers. Ingrid, if she remembered the name right. Entomologist, specializing in the rare moths found in the area. "I've seen him on television in San Diego. And sometimes he does special reports on the national news."

"Oh, yeah, maybe that's where I've seen him," another woman purred. Olivia, Sam guessed. Grad-student herpetologist. They'd introduced themselves to Sam when moving into the room next door.

There were other muffled, mostly female murmurs as the researchers trekked back and forth from the communal bathrooms to their dorm rooms on either side of Sam's. Then Adam must have exited the men's room, because the conversation seemed to centralize, with a lot of gushing tones. She heard Adam's lower register, and after he laughed, they all did, too.

Footsteps crunched across the gravel toward Sam's door,

and the doorknob turned.

Right outside, Olivia reminded Adam, "We're right next door!"

*Not for long*, Sam thought. She desperately wanted his help, but she didn't think she could tolerate twenty-four-hour togetherness with Adam Steele, especially in a small dormitory room.

"Christ," he grumbled, stepping into the room. "It *is* like frat life around here." He didn't sound truly displeased, though, and she supposed that any public figure never really got fed up with adoring fans.

Tomorrow she'd find someplace different for Adam to sleep. With luck, before Chase found out.

# 17

"And this is the remote canyon where Jade Silva's red CR-V was found, eight days after she failed to return to her room at the Southwestern Research Station in the Chiricahua Mountains." Adam looked directly at the camera, held by Dean, the crew member Adam had mentioned. The other member of Adam's crew, Alex, turned out to be a tall young woman with short brown hair, who held a tablet in her hands and seemed to be monitoring the sound from the tiny microphone clipped to Adam's shirt collar. Or maybe the video feed; Sam couldn't see over her shoulder.

"Although human blood was found in the cargo area of the car and her roommate, Summer Westin, has been trying to locate her for more than a week, local authorities simply don't seem interested in searching for Jade Silva."

Sam cringed. She'd asked him not to mention her participation at all.

"Isn't that right, Summer?"

The camera swung toward her. *Damn Adam.* She straightened, swallowed, and managed to mumble, "That's right."

How eloquent. Yeesh, they'd all hate her now—the border patrol, the county deputies, people she'd never even met. She added, "But I'm sure they're doing their best—"

At a gesture from Adam, the camera swung back to him. "Are they really?" He paused for a dramatic beat, then added, "Is Jade Luisa Silva's case being ignored because Jade is Hispanic-American?"

Sam chewed on her lower lip. Crap, what would Deputy Ortega or Agent Alvarez think of that question? A trickle of sweat ran down her forehead, and she marveled how Adam could manage to look so crisp on camera when she was quickly dissolving into a puddle in the harsh sunlight.

Adam continued, "Could Jade have mistakenly been picked up by ICE and now be held captive in a migrant detention center?"

*Yikes*. She hadn't even thought of that possibility.

"Or has Jade's story simply gotten lost in the flood of Hispanic migrants pouring over our southern border? The question remains . . ."

Another long pause as Adam's somber blue eyes locked dramatically on the camera, and he finally finished with, "What happened to Jade Silva?"

Next, he made a throat-slashing motion, and Dean lowered the camera.

"That's it?" Sam asked, disappointed. Jade's car had already been towed; there wasn't even any crime scene tape fluttering in the wind in the dry wash where the CR-V had been found.

"We'll start with the photo she sent you, a short segment about jaguars in Arizona, and some of the footage we took of the area this morning to show how desolate the region is."

"Good. And some information about how the border wall is bisecting the migration routes of jaguars and other animals?"

"Hmmm." Adam frowned slightly as he considered. "No. Jade's the real story, at least for tonight."

"Tonight?" Why did the thought of this story going on air send her gut into panic mode? "I thought you said you had four days to develop the story."

"And I thought you wanted to find your friend."

*Touché.* Sam didn't feel prepared for immediate exposure, but this was all for Jade's sake. And to showcase the plight of El Guapo and the other wildlife in the borderlands. Plus, she'd asked for it, hadn't she? "Tonight, then."

Adam nodded. "My station agreed to carry it on the six o'clock news."

Sam wasn't sure how much good a story about an Arizona case would do airing in San Diego. "Then we hope that the news ripples around the West?"

"No offense, but you're a troglodyte, Sammy." Adam chuckled. "No rippling. This story will spread like a match was dropped into a puddle of gasoline. This'll hit the news sites and YouTube and Twitter immediately after it airs back home. And then, after they see this, other stations will pick it up, a few as soon as the eleven o'clock tonight."

He wrapped an arm around her shoulders as they walked back to their cars. "I can't thank you enough for bringing me this. We've always made a great team, haven't we?"

Sam barely stopped herself from making an unladylike snort in response.

"What's next?" Adam turned to Alex, who was stroking a finger down her tablet, scrolling through the list of suggested tasks Sam had created for the reporter.

"We could go to the impound lot where they're keeping Silva's car," Alex suggested. "Or talk to the border patrol office in Douglas about an Agent"—she paused as she studied the note—"Landon In-hoff."

"*Im*hoff," Sam corrected.

Dean, Adam, and Alex all pivoted to look at her.

Adam asked, "Who's Imhoff? What does he have to do with this?"

"Maybe nothing," Sam told them. "But he went missing on the same day that Jade did. They found his patrol car parked in Douglas the next day."

She was grateful that Adam didn't ask how she knew that. As far as she was aware, the agent's disappearance had still not been advertised. When Sam had visited his apartment, Imhoff's fiancée Naomi had seemed concerned but uninformed. Surely by now she'd been told that Imhoff was missing. An internal investigation was probably ongoing, but it would no doubt be politically embarrassing for the border patrol to report to the public that one of their agents had simply walked off the job.

And there was no way she was going to say a word about the video clip with Imhoff's vehicle on it that Maria had shown her.

Adam weighed the choices, holding out his hands. "Impound lot," he said, lowering his left hand an inch. "Parked cars." Then he looked toward his right. "Border patrol. Missing agent who vanished the same day as our girl." He moved his right hand down toward his thigh as if he held a heavy weight. "No contest. Look out, border patrol, here we come! How far is Douglas from here?"

Alex consulted her tablet. "Looks like about an hour's drive."

"Good luck, guys. Please do *not* mention me." Sam spun toward her car.

"Wait!" Adam grabbed her sleeve. "Are you saying you're persona non grata with the border patrol? This could get juicy."

*Juicy?* She frowned. "I have no idea what you mean by that, and no, the border patrol won't even know my name. But

I don't need them knocking on my door to interview me about why I'm talking to the press about Imhoff."

Adam held her gaze for a long moment, then released her by blinking first. "Fair enough. You shall be a confidential source." He made a gesture like the pope blessing a pilgrim.

"This confidential source is headed back to the station," she told him. "Dinner duty."

"Again?" He unclipped the tiny microphone from his shirt collar and handed it to Alex, then pulled a handkerchief from his pocket and mopped his face.

"Until another helper arrives, I'm volunteering for two these days."

"Noble, but ugh." He grimaced. "See you later, then."

# 18

Adam showed up at the station at the tail end of dinner, but Bev rustled him up a plate of the remaining lasagna, salad, and cherry pie. She even put it all on a tray for him, with a folded napkin and a glass of iced tea. That sort of attention from Bev was a little shocking.

A cluster of admiring women flocked to Adam as soon as he sat down at one of the long tables. One of the women carried a tablet, and the group watched a replay of Adam's story, clucking over the mystery of Jade's disappearance and whether it was related to Imhoff's vanishing act. Several of them exclaimed about how good Adam looked on camera.

As Sam scrubbed down the other tables, she mused about what it would be like to go through life as a television celebrity. But she knew it hadn't always been this way for Adam. What would his fans think if they knew he'd been born Adam Steeke? That name didn't have quite the same cachet as Adam Steele.

After Bev had flicked the lights to urge the visitors out of the dining hall, a half dozen of the new researchers quizzed Sam across the counter as they dropped their dishes and tableware into the washing tubs between them.

"How do you know Adam Steele?" asked Amy, who looked to be mid-thirties, with dark hair in braids. Her turquoise T-shirt had a parrot on the front, so Sam guessed she was one of the ornithologists.

Sam responded with a vague "we're-old-friends" line.

"Is he going to be bunking with *you* from now on?" This came from Sam's next-dorm-room neighbor, grad student Olivia. The disbelief on the younger woman's face was a little insulting.

"We'll see." Sam smiled sweetly.

After she'd stacked the last clean dish on the counter for breakfast, Sam screwed up her courage and used the station landline to call Jade's mother. She'd already told Katerina about Jade's CR-V, and the poor woman would see Adam's report soon, if she didn't already know about it.

Katerina's voice was tense. "Do you think I should go to Bisbee?" she asked. "That's where the sheriff's office is, right? Or maybe Tombstone, because that's closer to where Jade's car was found? I don't know what I should do."

Sam tried to reassure the distraught mother. "I don't think there's anything you can do here, Katerina. At least not right now."

"And she might still be fine, right? Just because they found her car doesn't mean anything. Jade can hike for miles. I told you about the rhino."

Hadn't Katerina heard about the blood in Jade's CR-V? Clearly, she hadn't seen Adam's report tonight. Sam didn't intend to be the first to tell her, and she didn't want to offer trite reassurances to the poor woman. "I'm sure the authorities will call you when they find out anything more."

"A reporter called; he wants to interview me tomorrow. Do you think I should?"

"Was his name Adam Steele?"

"Yes. How did you know that?"

"He's a friend of mine. If you want to talk to him, you

should. It might help find Jade."

"That's a good idea. I will. I'll tell him about the rhino. Then everyone will understand how passionate my daughter is about wild animals. They'll see how she could get lost in the wilderness, and they'll all want to help look for her."

*Perfect*, Sam thought. Adam would tie the rhino story to the jaguar story in a poignant fashion; he had a flair for creating powerful dramas.

After returning to her dorm room, she worked on her articles, sorting out photos for each. She emailed Chase and Blake to tell them about Adam's involvement. At eight, she began to search the internet for Adam's story. He was right about the speed at which it would disseminate; his video was already posted on YouTube and airing on a streaming news channel. A few remarks in the response sections speculated that Jade was a Latina Lolita who had seduced the border patrol agent, or perhaps even killed him. But mostly, comments about the authorities' unfair treatment of Hispanic Americans were piling up like driftwood at high tide, along with the expected, nasty "Go back to where you came from" messages from a few malicious types. One of the most revolting responses came, ironically, from someone named Edward Rios. Had nobody ever told Ed that his last name was Hispanic?

She dithered about what to say to Maya, but before she could make up her mind, her internet exploration was interrupted by a video call from the nineteen-year-old. On the screen, Maya looked nearly hysterical. Her hair was a wild mess, and mascara drew dark lines down her cheeks as she angrily accused Sam of lying to her. "How could you, Sam? You knew I had to talk to her!"

"I'm sorry, Maya. I would have put the two of you in touch if I could have. I didn't know what to tell you, because I had no idea where Jade was. And I—we—still don't, so try to stay optimistic, okay?"

"But the car . . . and she's been missing for more than a week?"

Sam grimaced at the reminder. Today was actually the tenth day that Jade's location was unknown.

"And there's the border guard and cartels and people dying in the desert down there, and people locked up in those detention prisons . . ."

All true. As Sam watched her young friend sob and carry on, the screen began to blur as her own eyes filled with tears. She agreed with Maya that the outcome of Jade's saga did not seem likely to be a happy one. What could she say to this girl who had been thrilled to find a sister?

On the screen behind Maya, Sam spotted familiar objects: a Mexican serape over a blue couch, and a black-and-white cat sprawled in an easy chair. Simon. She ached to hold him; to listen to his purr. After Maya had dissolved into hiccupping sobs, a familiar pair of arms wrapped themselves around the teen, and Blake leaned down to add his face to the picture.

"I'm glad Maya's there with you, Blake," Sam said. "Take care of her."

She knew he would. Blake's daughter was only a few years younger than Maya, and he had a natural affection for both girls.

"Are you okay, Sam?" he asked.

She sniffed. "Mostly. I'll keep you posted. Or Adam will, on the news."

Maya blew her nose.

"I love you both," Sam said, "And—"

"Pet Simon for me," they chorused. Behind them, the cat lifted his head on hearing his name.

By the time she closed her laptop, Sam was so homesick

she could taste it. She carried her toiletry kit and towel to the communal bathroom, took a quick shower, and brushed her teeth. Only one other woman came in while she was standing in front of the sink, a redheaded student who seemed very shy and didn't even meet Sam's eyes. After using the toilet, she quickly slipped back out.

When Adam didn't show up in her room, Sam supposed he had driven down to Portal to stay with Dean and Alex. But he'd left his suitcase. It still lay open on Jade's desk, and a pair of pajama bottoms and his dopp kit lay on top of the bed.

Then she heard the low timbre of his voice amid female laughter in the adjoining dorm room.

Of course. She should have expected that.

At ten thirty, the partying next door quieted. Sam was reading in bed when Adam backed through the door, a wineglass in each hand. Sitting on the edge of her bed, he handed one to her. "You look like you could use this."

"Thanks." She wasn't a big fan of white wine, but she could use some alcoholic comfort right now. Taking a big gulp, she choked and gasped, fanning her face with a hand as the liquid seared its way down her throat. "This is tequila!"

Adam cocked an eyebrow. "Ever consider becoming a contestant on Jeopardy?"

Sam couldn't help chuckling. She took another sip, a smaller one this time. "Adam, are you still with ..." She couldn't remember the name of the woman Adam had been living with when she'd last talked to him.

"Kendra?" he supplied, sitting next to her on her bed.

She shook her head. "No, that wasn't it."

He took a sip from his glass, tried again, "Jeanette?"

"No, that's not right, either." Sam took another sip from her glass.

"Citronella?" He waved his glass in the air. "Chlamydia?"

They both dissolved into laughter.

After a quick tap, the door opened. Holly stood in the doorway, taking in the scene. "Having a good time?"

Oh yeesh, now she was going to be reprimanded for making noise after quiet hours. Sam propped herself up higher in bed as Adam told the head housekeeper, "I'm the one who deserves demerits, Holly. I'm leading Sam astray."

A tall man stepped around Holly and into the room. A man with raven hair and olive skin and a midnight shadow of beard darkening his cheeks and chin.

"Chase!" Sam set down her glass. She was out of her bed in a flash, sliding her arms around him, grazing her bicep on the shoulder holster under his left arm.

"Well, if it isn't the FBI." Adam leaned back on her bed, resting one arm on the mattress as he took another sip from his glass.

Chase leveled an index finger at the reporter. "You, out."

"Adam, we've got a room for you in the next building over," Holly hastened to explain, her voice cheerful again. "It's got a private bathroom and everything."

Grinning, Adam stood up, placed his wine glass on Jade's desk, and tossed the few items he'd dumped onto Jade's bed into his open suitcase. Then he zipped it up and wheeled it out the door. "See you at breakfast, amigos."

Before Holly closed the door, she murmured soberly to Sam, "You're officially the station slut now."

# 19

Sam managed to keep a straight face until the door clicked into place. Then she giggled and threw her arms around Chase's neck, leaping up and wrapping her legs around his hips. He staggered back a step, but managed to hold her by clasping his hands under her buttocks until he sat down, hard, on Jade's bed.

Between kisses, he said, "Stop that. I'm mad at you, you know."

"I know." She kissed him again.

"You taste like tequila," he commented when he came up for air.

"Join me." She handed him Adam's half-filled glass. "I'm so glad you're here, Chase. It's been sort of a shitty day. Sort of a shitty week, actually."

It was his turn to say, "I know."

"Except for the jaguar."

His lips twisted in a smile. "Of course, except for the jaguar." He took a sip of the tequila. "I remember there was an elegant something and a midget owl in this tale, too."

"Elegant trogon. Elf owl," she corrected. "Did you and Nicole wrap up your case?"

"A few details still need to be chased down, but the authorities in Las Vegas are cooperating and the federal district attorney in Washington State has filed charges," he told her. "Thankfully, it looks like only the casino manager knew money laundering was involved."

She guessed that Chase was happy about that because the casino manager was no doubt a tribal member. Chase was the FBI liaison between the tribes and the rest of the feds. All the other employees at the casino would likely be tribal members, too, so he would be glad to stay on good terms with the majority of them. Having been raised in the suburbs of Boise instead of on a reservation, Chase had always been insecure about the Native American half of his genes.

"Money laundering," she repeated. "Was it the mob?" She always thought of the mafia as money launderers, although she didn't have a good understanding of how that worked. Something about how funds coming in and going out didn't have a legitimate tie to the business they were supposedly passing through.

"Not the mob. But I can't talk about it, as you know."

She hated the way Chase ended so many conversations with a verbal slam of the door. Sam crossed the room to sit on her own bed again.

Upending his glass, Chase drained it. "Enough about my business. And by the way, it looks like Nicole may take a training assignment in Seattle. A trial separation from her husband."

Sam struggled to control her expression. That was the last thing she wanted, uber-sleek Nicole, on her own, within a two-hour drive of Chase's cabin.

Apparently, she didn't succeed with a poker face, because Chase said, "She was my work partner for years, Summer. We are friends. We'll always be good friends."

"I understand," Sam told him. "It's kind of like me and Adam."

He gave her a dark look. "It's *nothing* like you and Steele. That man would kiss you one minute and toss you off a cliff the next if it would make a dramatic news story."

She grinned at the description. "That's probably true."

"Is this bed taken?" Chase patted Jade's bunk.

"Not anymore. But there's plenty of room in this one, too." She stroked her hand over her mattress.

"I was hoping you'd say that." Grinning, he unbuttoned his shirt.


When she woke to the sounds of birdsong outside the window, Sam's heart felt several pounds lighter than it had yesterday. Slipping quietly from her bed, she gathered her toiletries, towel, and clothes for a trip to the women's restroom. Chase was still snoring in Jade's bed, but they'd made slow, sweet love for nearly an hour before they agreed that there was no way to actually sleep on top of each other in a twin.

When she returned, fully clothed, Chase was awake. He pushed himself up against the wall, cushioning his back with a pillow. "Where are you going?"

When she bent to kiss him, he waved her away. "No fair. You're all minty. I have dragon breath."

She settled for kissing his brow. "Volunteer duty calls, and I've been doing both my shift and Jade's until someone else gets recruited. I'm on the roster for breakfast."

"When does that finish?"

"I should be done washing dishes around eight thirty."

"Good," he said. "We need to go to Tucson after that."

"Tucson?" That city was more than two hours away and nowhere close to where Jade had disappeared. Sam was not scheduled to leave for another three weeks. "Remember that I drove here from Bellingham. You're not putting me on a plane, if that's what you have in mind."

He shook his head. "Nothing like that."

"I'm sticking this out until Jade is found."

"This might have to do with Jade, Summer."

She waited, her hand on the doorknob.

Chase flapped a hand at her. "Go. I'll explain later."

As she pulled the door open, cold dawn air wafted in. "You'll hear the breakfast bell at seven, and you'll want to line up with everyone else right away. Mealtimes here are akin to a horde of locusts descending at harvest."

"Got it." Peeling down the sheet, he slid out of bed.

The sight of his lean, naked body made it hard to leave for the dining hall.

As she flitted back and forth from the eating area to the kitchen, she noticed Adam charming his usual cluster of groupies with a tale about reporting live on a coast guard drug bust in San Diego Bay.

Chase had attracted several young female researchers, too. He wasn't holding court, though, just answering questions about who he was and asking the women about themselves in return.

Before leaving the research station with Chase, Sam conferred briefly with Adam about the day's schedule.

"I've got interviews with the border patrol in Douglas in ninety minutes, then with Jade's mother at one," he told her.

She checked her watch. "You'll never make it to Santa Fe by one. It's at least a six-hour drive."

Adam stood up. "That's why we'll be flying there from Douglas. And back again." His confident grin reminded her that they lived in very different worlds now.

"With that kind of mobility, you might also consider interviewing my friend Diego Xintal."

"Who's he?"

"The jaguar expert I hiked with to find El Guapo—that's

the name of that jaguar in Jade's photo. Spanish for 'The Handsome One.'"

"I know what it means; half the population of California speaks Spanish, you know. But the answer is no on Shint-whatever, at least for the moment. We need to keep the focus on Jade right now. I might look up Imhoff's fiancée in Douglas, however, if I get back at a reasonable hour."

Chase strode over to tug on her sleeve, reminding her that they needed to hit the road.

"Speaking of that, Adam, Chase and I might be back late, too."

Chase added, "Or not until tomorrow morning."

Sam gave him a questioning look.

Adam glanced from Chase to Sam. "What're you two up to?"

"None of your business," Chase told him.

"Sam?" Adam's gaze implored her for an answer.

"I don't know either," she said. "But I'll share if it's important."

"I'm counting on that." Pulling his jacket from the back of his chair, Adam headed for the exit.

She turned back to Chase. "What do you mean, we might not be back tonight?"

"It depends. If things go too late, we might want to spend the night in Tucson." He rubbed his neck. "In a full-size bed, in a nice hotel."

"I'd better warn Bev, then." She pivoted toward the kitchen.

Chase grabbed her arm. "I already told the whole staff. And I took the liberty of packing some overnight stuff for you, just in case."

Sam fumed at the way he'd taken over, but she allowed Chase to shepherd her to his rental car. On the nearly three-hour drive, he insisted on hearing about everything she'd done in her quest to find Jade. He quizzed her at every turn about exactly what she'd seen and who said what. When she got to the stories of the plastic-wrapped parcel in the rock cleft and the Patriot Posse wake-up call, Chase's hands tightened on the steering wheel, his knuckles white. She knew that he was reliving his own nightmare as an undercover agent with a militia group a few years ago. He'd come close to dying.

They were nearing the outskirts of Tucson when she finally concluded, "And so, then I called Adam."

Chase shook his head. "Jesus, Summer, the things you get yourself involved in."

Annoyed, she replied, "Hey, I *planned* to spend six weeks washing dishes for free room and board in a gorgeous place where I could explore the mountains and write articles about the incredible ecosystems of the Sky Islands. How was I to know that my roommate would be a talented wildlife photographer who would vanish after she sent me a priceless photo?"

His gaze remained on the road as he said, "You could have left it up to the authorities to investigate."

"The authorities weren't interested in investigating." Hadn't she already said that a dozen times?

"It's a wonder you're still alive. This is not a good time to go wandering around the border area, and I know you've heard enough to realize that."

He was stalling. She'd had it with the suspense. "Where the hell are you taking me, Chase?"

"We're here." He pulled the car into a parking spot in front of a low, nondescript building. A sign in front proclaimed it OFFICE OF THE PIMA COUNTY CORONER.

"Coroner?" She grabbed his arm. "Chase, what do you know that I don't?"

He exhaled heavily. "It's just a hunch, and believe me, I hope I'm wrong, *querida*. But this office provides autopsy services for Cochise County, and they keep records of all the migrants found throughout southeast Arizona."

"*Dead* migrants, you mean."

He swallowed. "Yes. More than two hundred have been found this year. Twenty-three just in the time frame since Jade disappeared."

"Oh, God." She stared at the building in horror.

But she had to know. She reached for the door handle.

The female clerk that the receptionist hailed to assist them seemed nice. She offered coffee or a soft drink while she installed Sam in front of a computer in a small room off the lobby. "These are the possibles," she said gently as she brought up a PDF file on the screen. "Use the arrow keys to move from one photo to the next."

Sam stared inanely at the keyboard, not wanting to touch it.

The clerk spoke to Chase. "They're in two-page spreads, photo on the left, description on the right."

"Thank you," Chase told her.

The clerk closed the door behind her as she left.

Chase pulled a chair up next to Sam. "You okay?"

"Of course not." She glared at the title page of the PDF, simply labeled Pima County Coroner, followed by the date range from the day of Jade's disappearance to today.

"Let's begin." Chase touched the right arrow key, and the on-screen page turned, displaying a photo of a young girl, clearly deceased. Her face was purple, swollen, and blotchy, her eyes and mouth half-open, her tongue visible between cracked lips.

"Crap." Sam groaned. "She can't be more than ten."

Chase pointed to the description on the facing page.

"Estimated seven to nine years of age. Unidentified. Died of exposure. Found on the Tohono O'odham Reservation."

The page included height and weight and other details about the girl's body, but there was no point in reading that grim information. What was this girl's story? Who had left her to die in the desert?

"Next." Chase pressed the key again.

"Oh, they included men too," Sam remarked, looking at the next display: a young man, thin, his lips dried and curled above crooked teeth, a small cross in one pierced earlobe.

"*Carajo!* I asked them to sort these out." Chase reached for the screen.

Sam slapped his hand aside. "I want to see them. All of them. They deserve that much." She read from the screen, "Identification card in wallet. Cecil Quichocho, 26, from Tegucigalpa, Honduras." She turned to Chase. "Why would they include the ones who've been identified?"

"Some of the documents might be fake," Chase guessed. Reading from the screen, he stated, "Head injury, blunt force trauma."

"Meaning he was murdered?" she asked.

"Or fell and hit his head on a rock."

Sam pressed the key to continue.

Plowing through the pages was such a sad, horrific task. How many relatives and friends had done this in the last several years? Some corpses were tentatively named by papers found with them; others were simply labeled "Unidentified." Some were children, one only a couple of years old. Had the kids died during the journey and their bodies been left unclaimed because their parents were illegal immigrants? Sam couldn't imagine what it felt like to have a child die on a journey to find a better life.

Her heart hurt. She felt like wailing, "Why do they keep

coming?" just like Dulcie Thorensen had. Wiping away tears from her eyes, she kept turning the pages.

One man appeared to be Middle Eastern, not Hispanic, and the file included two women who were obviously Asian. Had these people joined groups of migrants from Mexico and Central America, or had they come on their own?

A fair-haired man's photo stood out among the dozens of darker-skinned, black-haired deceased. He had sandy-brown hair in a buzz cut, a thin mustache on his upper lip. Sam slowly scrutinized his swollen face, which was severely sunburned. Blisters covered his cheeks and lips, even extending down onto his neck. His eyes were half-open.

"What?" Chase asked, curious about why she'd paused on the photo.

"He looks familiar." Unidentified, found in the desert outside of Bisbee, wearing only army-green cargo pants.

"He died of a gunshot wound to the chest," Chase observed. "Found in a canyon north of Bisbee. He was probably involved in illegal activity, ran afoul of a cartel or something like that. It's unlikely you two would ever have crossed paths."

"I know I've seen him before," Sam insisted. Had she seen him in Bisbee before he died? Then it came to her. The photo of the happy couple in Naomi's apartment. "Oh crap, Chase; this is Landon Imhoff, the missing border patrol agent!"

"Are you sure?"

"I saw his photo in his apartment."

"You were in his apartment? You didn't tell me that."

Sam gave him a dark look, then watched as Chase pulled out the pocket notebook he carried everywhere and made a note.

*Oh God, poor Naomi.* Sam hoped Landon's fiancée had given birth in the past few days so she'd have someone she loved to cling to when she received this news. What could have happened for Imhoff's patrol truck to end up in Douglas and his body outside of Bisbee? She thought about the grim conversations she'd overheard among the Broads, about the brutality of the cartels. But that discussion had been about severed heads and corpses left in public places. If Imhoff's stripped and discarded body was meant to send a message, it seemed like that message could only be that the agent was as worthless as all the migrants on these other pages.

The next two images were of women. It was difficult to tell their ages because of the damage to the skin on their faces. It looked as if birds had been at their corpses. Tohono O'odham Reservation again. She'd seen it on the map; the reservation covered a vast area of Arizona desert, and the tribal members lived on both sides of the border.

Number twenty-two. An older woman. Probably someone's beloved grandma, unable to walk so far, so fast, over such rough terrain in such brutal heat.

She was almost to the end of the heartbreaking photos. Sam pressed the key again, and the photo of a dark-haired woman appeared.

"No," she said in a quiet voice. "No."

"Unidentified," Chase read from the description. "Wearing cargo pants and a stained men's T-shirt, apparently put on her body after death, because when the shirt was removed, the coroner found two bullet wounds in her chest. She was discovered only a mile or so from that border patrol agent. So maybe they both ran afoul of a drug deal gone wrong."

Turning her face away from the screen, Sam lowered her head into her hands. "No, no, no!"

Chase gently rested his hand on the back of her neck. "Did you know her?"

"That's Jade." She sat up again, her gaze fixed in horror on the image of her dead roommate. She wanted to scream, throw a hysterical fit, vomit. But she was paralyzed, her brain and gut aching. Her body felt as if it could shatter any second.

"Okay." After making a note, Chase switched off the monitor. Jade's face vanished from the screen. He wrapped his arms around Sam and pulled her close. "Okay."

# 20

Sam was grateful that Chase took on the tasks of reserving a hotel room in Tucson and calling the authorities. And although it made her feel like a coward, she let him notify the staff at the research station and Jade's mother, too. As she listened to that last call, she noticed that Chase didn't tell Katerina how her daughter had died. No parent would want to hear that their child had been shot to death.

As Sam paced in the hotel room, sipping her second glass of wine, her sorrow slowly changed to anger. This wasn't some accidental death by exposure, getting lost in the desert in the heat of the day. Jade hadn't fallen off a cliff or been bitten by a rattlesnake. And neither had Agent Imhoff. They'd been murdered. Their deaths were still linked somehow.

There wouldn't be a happy ending, but Sam was determined that Jade's murder would be solved. So she did the most useful thing she could think of to do at the moment. She went into the bathroom, closed the door between her and Chase, and called Adam.

To Adam's credit, he made all the appropriate noises of sympathy at her news, but there was no mistaking the excitement that crept into his voice.

"I'm across town right now," he told her.

"Weren't you going to Santa Fe? And Douglas?" Then she

remembered. "Oh yeah, the private plane."

"Yep. So I'll get out to the coroner's office before they close. This will make tonight's news, I guarantee it."

"Be sure to ask the public for any information, any clues they might have."

"Of course, babe. Thanks for calling me right away."

She was afraid he was going to reiterate what a great team they made, but Adam only said, "I'm so sorry it ended this way."

"Me too." She stifled a sob.

After ending the call, she stared at her cell phone. One call left to make, and she was the only one who could make it. Maya. Taking a deep breath and wiping the tears from her cheeks, she tapped the girl's number in her contact list.

"Do you have some news?" Maya sounded breathless.

"Are you still with Blake?"

"Yeah, I'm at your place. That noise you hear is Blake banging around in the kitchen."

"I'm *cooking*!" her housemate's voice insisted in the background. "Is that Sam?"

"Can you put me on speaker?" she asked Maya.

"You're on." Maya's voice now sounded more distant. "I'm putting you on the counter between us."

There was no postponing it. "I have sad news, Maya."

"Shit!" Maya shrieked. "Shit, shit, shit! Jade's dead, isn't she?" Her voice cracked on the word "dead," and Sam could hear her young friend starting to hyperventilate in the background.

Sam could find no way to soften the news. If she were only religious like her father, she might be able to say something about "God's plan" or "in a better place" or something, anything, that could make the girl feel better. But if two bullets to a young woman's chest were God's plan, she didn't want anything to do with that cruel deity. "Yes, Maya, today we found out Jade died in the desert."

For several moments, Sam heard nothing but sobs and shrieks and soft murmurs from Blake. Then, finally, Jade demanded, "How? How did she die, Sam?"

"She was murdered. She had been shot."

More choking sobs, then a gasp for breath. "Who killed her?"

"I don't know, Maya. But I swear that I'll do my best to find out." Although she knew it wouldn't make any difference at this point, she couldn't help saying, "I will always care about you, Maya. I love you."

After another painful moment of listening to the girl's cries and choking back sobs of her own, Sam added, "Blake, I love you, too. Please take care of Maya. I wish I could be there."

The speaker echo ended as her housemate picked up the phone. "You take care of yourself, you hear, Sam?"

She sniffed. "I'll be okay. Chase is here with me."

"Good."

"And Adam, too."

"That should be interesting."

"Yeah," she agreed. "But I need him. Jade needs Adam's skills now, more than ever. Prepare Maya to hear the story on the news."

"I will. And we'll both pet Simon tonight. Your cat may be bald by the time you come back."

His ending words made her smile even through her tears.

# 21

The public outrage following Adam's report on the deaths of Jade Silva and Landon Imhoff shook southern Arizona like an earthquake. Even the national news was filled with conflicting discussions about needing more law enforcement in the borderlands and accusations that the militarization of the area was the cause of so many needless deaths. Curiously, the vigilantes were never mentioned.

The next afternoon, Chase drove Sam from Tucson back to the research station because she insisted on fulfilling her volunteer contract. He spent the night with her in the dorm room, holding her in his arms, but in the morning, he told her he needed to return to Las Vegas.

"I'm sorry," he apologized, kissing the top of her head as they stood by the door.

"I expected that." She lifted her face for a goodbye kiss. "I'll be fine."

"Summer, please leave the investigation to the professionals."

She gritted her teeth, exasperated. "Chase, at this stage, I probably know more than they do."

"That might be true, but don't forget that the murderers are still out there." When she didn't respond, he frowned and then added, "At least keep law enforcement in the loop, okay?

That includes me. Call me tonight. Around nine?"

"Have a safe trip back to Vegas. Say hi to Nicole for me." She shut the door behind him.

Sam spent the rest of the day mowing the lawn and doing kitchen chores and even helping to repair a bridge over a local stream, anything to keep her body occupied while her brain raged about Jade's murder. In the late afternoon, she received an email from Adam, telling her to watch his special report on the national news that night. After searching the internet, she finally found a site that was streaming it live and tuned in just as he was summarizing the murders of Jade and Imhoff.

"They both died from gunshot wounds. But at whose hands? Drug smugglers? Human traffickers? Desperate migrants?" he asked the camera. "The borderlands are in dangerous turmoil right now. Is the wall making the situation worse or better? I'm here with ranchers Eli and Jacob MacGregor to hear their opinion on this."

The picture widened to show two middle-aged men in western-style shirts, jeans, and cowboy hats standing nearby. In the background was a pole barn, and in the distance, a bollard section of the border wall rippled over sandy, brush-covered hills.

"Our family has owned this land for nearly a century," Eli said in response to Adam's prompt. "We used to get along with everyone on the Mexican side, and we still do for the most part."

"But in recent years," his brother Jacob chimed in, "we've had a flood of Mexicans crossing our property. They leave trash and take the water out of our troughs. And they've even killed a couple of our calves and eaten them. And sometimes we find 'em out there, lost and begging for help. Or dead."

"So far this year, we've found six bodies on the ranch," Eli volunteered.

"So, you understandably wanted the federal government to help," Adam stated.

"Yeah, we wanted them to stop all the illegals. But we didn't ask for the feds to grab our land." He pointed to the wall in the distance. "That fence is not on the border. More than three hundred acres of our ranch are on the other side, and half our water supply."

"By putting the wall there, the feds just gave 'em to Mexico," the other brother summarized. "Said, here you go, *amigos*. Didn't pay us, either."

Adam asked, "You received no remuneration from the government for your land?"

Jacob confirmed, "Nope, we got no money. They say this is a national security issue, so they don't have to."

"See, it's something called the Real ID Act," Eli said. "Bush Junior enacted it after 9-11, and according to the border patrol, it trumps every other law. So now the feds can just do whatever they feel like."

"Interesting," Adam commented. "Does the wall help to keep the migrants off your ranch?"

"Slows 'em down, I guess," Eli admitted. "But they just build ladders or go under or cut holes. They got all the same tools in Mexico that we do. Hell, one time I found a big fishing net strung up over the fence down there. The border patrol can't get around fast enough to catch them all. You heard me say we already found six dead ones this year. There could be more out there right now." He gazed beyond the camera into the distance.

His brother pointed the other way, toward the wall. "That section you're looking at right there cost millions. Millions! Hell, if the government gave *us* those millions, we could hire guards to sit there 24-7."

"So, you're not happy about having the wall on your

property?" Adam asked.

"It's supposed to be on the *border*," Jacob emphasized. "Not wherever they damn well feel like putting it." He pushed his cowboy hat back on his head, suddenly looking chagrined. "Oops. Can I say damn on the air?"

Adam smiled. "You sure can. Eli and Jacob MacGregor are ranchers on the southern Arizona border. Thank you for helping us understand a little more about what it's like to live and work down here."

The camera focused again on Adam as he peered intently into the lens, his expression sober. "I'm Adam Steele, with an exclusive report from the troubled Arizona borderlands."

As Sam switched over to email, she felt proud of having brought Adam into the mix. She hoped that he had started his report with the jaguar photo again and a sentence or two about how the wall disrupted wildlife migration and how Jade had cared about that. But even if he hadn't, Sam admired the way Adam was fearlessly tackling all the issues down here. She hadn't said a word to him about ranchers because she hadn't spoken to a single one; he'd chased that lead down all on his own. Maybe she should send him to the Straubs for their story. If the public wasn't concerned about wildlife, maybe they'd care about property rights.

She called Adam, and was surprised when he answered his cell. "Hi, babe. I have about two minutes, then I gotta run."

"Adam, I just want to tell you that I think you're absolutely fantastic."

"I've been telling you that for years." She could hear the smile in his voice.

"You've really got guts to air all these critical ideas. I'm surprised you're not getting blowback."

He laughed. "Oh, I'm getting plenty of that. Even death threats from the pro-wall groupies."

"What? You're kidding."

"That's their standard reaction to any criticism. Next they'll be trying to deport me, or holding rallies where they shout 'String him up!'"

"You can joke, but now I'm really worried, Adam. I know from personal experience there are true believers with guns wandering around down here. I told you about my run-in with those Patriot Posse guys."

"Vigilantes! That's a great idea. I'll see if Alex can unearth a few militia types to interview tomorrow before we leave. Thanks!"

*Yeesh.* Well, she'd asked for it, hadn't she? "You haven't heard anything from law enforcement about Jade's case, have you? Or Imhoff's?"

"No. And if you do, I'm counting on you to share."

"I will."

"I hear there's a growing memorial down at the wall where Jade took the photo. My crew will be there tomorrow morning at ten. You should come, too."

"I will. I'd like to see that."

"Gotta run, babe. Stay cool." And Adam was gone.

She and Chase chatted after that via internet video. Sam was painfully aware of cool, sleek, sophisticated Nicole by Chase's side, her makeup perfect. Sam's face was sunburned and sweaty and more than once during their conversation, tears rolled down her blotchy cheeks.

According to Chase, clues were flying into the law enforcement tip lines. "Most are completely useless, of course," he told her. "But a forest service ranger showed up with something that might prove useful."

Sam perked up, desperate for any shred of evidence.

"She brought in a cell phone that she found while sorting through the garbage for recyclable cans and bottles. It has the letters *JLS* on the back."

"Jade Luisa Silva," Sam told him.

"Unfortunately, the front was cracked and the back was missing, and so was the SIM card. We can't get into it."

Her heart fell. "You're telling me about a dead end?"

"There could be prints, of course, so it's being processed. I had my Arizona colleagues send it to the FBI lab, and maybe they can tap into the memory, too."

Sometimes it was useful to have the feds involve themselves. They usually had better resources than local law enforcement, and political pressure could make things move more quickly.

"If the data is recoverable," Chase continued, "the memory could contain contacts and maybe some photos and messages. Or it's possible that she used the cloud to store images."

Knowing how protective Jade could be about her photos, Sam doubted that. "Fingers crossed," she told him.

"Mine, too, Summer. And the blood tests from the lab are back. Both Jade's blood and Imhoff's were found in the cargo area of Jade's CR-V."

She groaned. "Does that mean they were tossed in there? Someone else was driving?"

"That's the likely scenario. There are someone else's prints on the steering wheel and seat adjustment lever, but they don't match any in the database. But the cartels routinely grab new slaves off the streets every day. Or maybe they pressured a migrant into doing their dirty work."

"Just so you know, Chase, Jade wouldn't be involved in anything drug-related. She didn't even drink."

"Then maybe she was just in the wrong place at the wrong time. I know this doesn't help much right now, but I wanted you to know that the authorities *are* working on this."

"Thanks for telling me."

"How are you holding up?"

"I'm hanging in, just hunkering down and working. Tomorrow, my article about Jade and El Guapo and the Sky Island habitats will come out in the digital version of *Wild America* magazine. The photo of the jaguar at the wall will be the front cover. The print version will arrive everywhere in a few days."

"That's fantastic! You should be proud."

*Wild America* was the winner of what had become a bidding war after Jade's death was announced. They weren't the bidder offering the biggest price, but they were the only publication promising to keep the focus on Jade's passion for wildlife, and they'd include the details about habitats being sliced in two by the border wall. Other publications wanted to edit out the wildlife issues and focus on Jade as a Hispanic-American. Sam had signed contracts to write articles for two magazines about her experiences searching for Jade in the borderlands. But the jaguar-at-the-wall photo belonged only to Adam's television network and *Wild America* for a period of one year.

The money was great and Sam was happy that the story would get attention, but somehow, she felt dirty, like she'd unfairly benefited from Jade's death. She planned to donate everything she could afford to conservation groups.

"Tomorrow I'm going down to the wall," she told Chase. "Adam's coming, too, with his crew. He tells me there's a growing memorial there."

"Be careful."

She was tired of his constant warnings about staying safe. "Bye, Chase."

"Till tomorrow, *querida*."

# 22

Nobody knew where Jade Silva had died, so the section of the wall where she had taken the jaguar photograph became a shrine. Adam told her that the pile of flowers and cards grew daily, and Sam wanted to see for herself. According to Chase, the top brass of the border patrol wanted to discourage the public attention and pilgrimages, but apparently agents had been told to leave the visitors and the display alone, at least for now. Although they'd planted a huge DO NOT BLOCK ROAD sign next to the wall, the green-striped SUVs simply drove past the area without stopping.

Sam planned to donate to a wildlife cause in Jade's name instead of adding to the bouquets wilting in the heat, but viewing the number of flowers and cards left there still warmed her heart. So many strangers cared about Jade's death.

She arrived a little after 9:00 a.m., before Adam and his crew. As she approached the location, an older man and woman were placing something on the growing display. Another woman was kneeling in the dirt. Sam parked alongside the road, behind a small tan pickup and a green Audi, and walked across the gravel to examine the memorial.

Someone had enlarged Jade's photo from the paper and then framed it and wired it to the mesh panel at eye level.

Beneath Jade's image was a hill of scented candles and notes and prayer cards and other tokens, like a jaguar beany baby toy, as well as dozens of bouquets. Some visitors had fastened notes to the fence with twist ties. A few notes attached with tape were rapidly peeling away from the metal; as Sam watched, one dropped to the ground like a dying butterfly.

"Summer?"

She turned. The older woman held out a hand in her direction, but didn't actually touch her. "I'm so sorry you lost Jade."

Sam recognized the couple now. The Straubs, from the Earthship house.

"Carl and I were hoping for a better outcome," Frannie said.

"I was, too." Sam bit her lip.

"Goddamn cartels with their drug trafficking," Carl muttered, frowning fiercely.

Sam thought about challenging his comment, about saying that Jade could have been killed for other reasons, by other people. She was troubled that the locals so readily accepted the cartel explanation. They were the same people who'd told her the cartels liked to display their kills to warn others, and Jade's body had been hidden in the desert. A cartel killing also didn't explain why Agent Imhoff had been killed and discarded along with Jade. But then, nothing about the murders made sense to Sam.

A border patrol vehicle passed, showering them with dust. The lone agent inside did not even glance in their direction.

"Goddamn patrol. Goddamn wall." Behind his thick glasses, Carl's gaze flicked up and down the structure as if he might be able to scowl it away.

Frannie tugged on his arm, and the Straubs returned to their pickup. The rifle hung above the back window, and Sam wondered again whether Carl could clearly see what he fired at. The elderly couple seemed nice, but maybe she should suggest to the sheriff's deputies that they check the Straubs' rifle.

She turned sadly back to the wall. The kneeling woman Sam had noticed when she arrived was a couple of yards away, her face hidden beneath a floppy sun hat. She appeared to be praying.

Most of the cards at the wall contained the common, traditional "Gone Too Soon" and "Forever in Our Hearts" types of messages, but two implied that the writers shared Jade's passion: "Goodbye, Wildlife Warrior" and "RIP, Jaguar Girl." Another was a print of the now-famous jaguar-at-the-wall photo, with the words "This is Murder!" splashed across the top in red marker. Sam wasn't sure whether the statement was meant to indicate Jade or the jaguar. She supposed it really didn't matter.

Bending over the pile of items left behind, Sam slid aside a wilted rose to pick up the folded note beneath. "We hope you're in a better, kinder place now.—Carl and Frannie Straub." That wish was probably as much for their future as for Jade's.

The kneeling woman clutched at the fence and pulled herself to her feet, holding a card in one hand. Sam shot a sideways glance at her, wondering whether she'd known Jade. When she raised her head and Sam could see beneath the drooping rim of the hat, Sam was surprised that her face seemed familiar. It took a moment to place the memory. RTK Construction. Phil Thorensen's wife, Dulcie.

She met Sam's gaze, and Sam could see a spark of recognition in the other woman's eyes. Mrs. Thorensen said, "Hello, again."

"Hello again," Sam responded, taking a few steps in her direction. What had Thorensen called her? Dulcie, that was it.

Dulcie's eyes gleamed with unshed tears. "I'm sorry about your friend." She hesitated, holding out her free hand.

Sam briefly took Dulcie's fingers in her own. "Thank you." It always seemed so pointless to thank someone for sympathy, but she'd been taught to be polite by her preacher father.

Dulcie looked toward the makeshift memorial again. She wiped the back of her hand across her eyes, but a tear rolled down her cheek and plopped onto the card she held. "Oh." She brushed at the damp spot, then set the card down on top of a stuffed jaguar before straightening again. "She was young and idealistic, wasn't she?"

"Yes, she was." Sam had no tears left. Now, her chest simply ached with sorrow and tension. That very real pain was probably the source of the word "heartache." But what was the term for the burn of anger in her gut? Jade's death was a tragedy, but not an accident.

"Can I show you something?" Dulcie swung the purse from her shoulder. She extracted a billfold and pulled it open to show Sam a photo of a girl who looked about the same age as Maya. With strong features and chin-length brown hair, she wasn't exactly pretty, but her direct stare was arresting. "This is our daughter, Brooke."

Sam nodded, unsure how to respond. "I see."

"She's a sophomore at Arizona State. And these"—she thumbed the photo sleeve over to reveal two lookalike boys in side-by-side images—"are Luke and Liam. They'll be freshmen this fall."

Sam wanted to say, *Aren't you lucky they're alive,* but made herself demurely remark, "You must be proud of them."

"We are." Dulcie snapped her wallet shut and replaced it in her purse. "We never dreamed we'd be able to send all three of them to college, but now . . ." After a quick glance at the wall, she let the rest of the sentence dissipate into the hot air.

"Well, I'd better be going. You take care."

"I will. Bye." Sam watched as the other woman walked across the road and opened the trunk of a metallic green Audi sedan. Dulcie extracted a can of Coke from a small cooler there, wiping the top with a rag she pulled from a bag that looked as if it contained discarded clothing.

Sam remembered the car because it had been the only non-white non-truck in the RTK lot, and it had a distinctive Z-shaped blemish on the far-left side of the front bumper, as if the driver had swiped something while turning. Probably while trying to work a way out of that jumble of heavy trucks.

A border patrol vehicle was churning up dust on the hill to the east, and it soon arrived, towing two tires behind it on long ropes. The SUV plowed to a stop beside Sam. The window on her side rolled down, and Agent Alvarez peered out. Agent Bradley was in shadow in the driver's seat, but she could see that his face was turned toward her, too.

"Hello, guys," Sam said tentatively.

"Are we *ever* going to get rid of you?" Alvarez asked.

She had no response to that, and no idea what was going through the agents' minds. "Sorry about Agent Imhoff," she finally said. Was there a memorial somewhere for him?

"Yeah, well." Alvarez faced the road again. "Have a nice day." His window rolled up, and the SUV plowed onward.

Another large vehicle passed. The taco truck. Sam held up a hand to acknowledge the driver. In response, he raised his middle finger before blowing on past. Sam wished Taco Lobo four flat tires in the near future.

Less than a minute after Adam and his crew arrived, three teenage girls drove up in a Jeep. One carried a teddy bear, another a heart-shaped balloon, the third a stack of cards. That girl, Celinda Ibarra, told Adam that the cards had been written by her Sunday school class. The three girls were overly effusive, so thrilled to be interviewed by Adam on camera that Sam wondered whether these poignant television moments had been planned.

While Adam chatted with the teens, a small elderly man arrived. His skin was coffee brown, his face lined and leathery. Sam watched as he carefully unwrapped and deposited a stone figure of a jaguar at the edge of the shrine, scraping out a flat space to set down the carving. Standing alongside the cameraman, Dean, Sam caught Adam's attention and silently pointed to the old man.

Adam immediately shifted his attention to the elder, much to the disappointment of the girls.

"I was born in Yucatan," the old man told Adam. He refused to look directly at the camera but was willing to talk. "My mother is Mayan, my father a Zapotec. The jaguar is sacred to both my cultures. We call him *el tigre*. And *el tigre* was here." He turned, placed both hands reverently on the wire mesh and briefly touched his forehead to the rust-colored metal, his lips moving as if he whispered a prayer. Then he looked at Adam and said, "May *el tigre* protect that girl who loved jaguars, Jade Silva, in the afterlife. And may he devour the soul of the one who killed her."

Sam couldn't have said it better herself.

She wasn't surprised when Adam simply nodded, faced the camera, and closed out his report.

# 23

Two days later, a memorial service was held for Jade Silva in Santa Fe. Katerina Franco didn't want to wait for a resolution to her daughter's murder. The urn that would eventually contain Jade's cremated remains was ornate silver with turquoise inlays. It sat on a high table in the front of the hall, flanked by photographs of Jade as a child and as a young woman. One photo showed Jade with a black-haired man who had to be Lorenzo Silva. His lips had the same bow-shaped contour and his almond-shaped eyes were the same as Jade's. And as Maya's.

Although she sat demurely in the pew beside Sam, Maya's gaze remained fixed on those photos. Sorrow radiated from the teenager in a cloud so thick and painful that Sam could practically see it.

Mounted on the wall above and behind the memorial table, was a video screen featuring a slow, continuous slideshow of Jade's amazing wildlife photographs. One was of a dragonfly on a leaf, both the insect and the vegetation made jewel-like by tiny pearls of dew.

Indicating the photo, Sam told Maya. "That's what I meant by artistry."

"Katerina told me Jade took that when she was only six years old," a woman at the end of the pew murmured to the man beside her.

Sam had no difficulty in spotting Jade's mother. The beautiful woman sobbing into a handkerchief in the front row, with shoulder-length silver-threaded dark hair and Jade's olive skin, had to be Katerina Franco. The gray-haired man next to her, her second husband.

Several people glanced curiously back and forth between the photo of Jade in the front of the room and Maya, sitting quietly in a pew. Discreet finger-pointing and hushed whispers behind hands indicated that some people had noted the remarkable resemblance.

Sam had told Jade's mother that she was coming, but she hadn't warned Katerina that she'd have her deceased husband's "love child" by her side. Maya, usually so ready with snappy comebacks, so good at rolling with all the brutal punches life had thrown at her, remained absolutely devastated by Jade's death. She'd never even had a chance to meet her supposed half sister before Jade was gone. The teen's doppelganger, her kindred spirit and perhaps her sole relative, her new role model, had been abruptly snuffed out like a candle flame in a rainstorm. Maya herself seemed like a ghost right now.

During the service, Sam kept a hand pressed hard to her mouth to stifle her sobs as tears streamed down her cheeks. She had to blow her nose twice, causing others in the pew to stare at her in irritation or sympathy. Next to her, Maya sat pale and silent, her lips clamped into a thin line as tears dripped down her face.

As they approached the church exit after the service, Sam fretted about what might happen next. At the door, she took Katerina's hand in hers. "I'm Sam Westin. I'm so sorry for your loss."

"The roommate. Thank you for looking for Jade. Thank

you for caring about my daughter." Katerina embraced her in a brief hug that left a lump in Sam's throat.

Based on what Jade had told her about her mother, Sam worried that Katerina might freak out on seeing a young woman who looked so much like the daughter she'd just lost. Sucking in a deep breath for courage, Sam held out a hand to Maya, who was hiding in the crowd behind her. Grasping the girl's fingers, she towed Maya forward to meet Jade's mother. "Katerina, this is—"

"My God in heaven." As Katerina stared at Maya, the older woman abruptly went pale, and her eyes filled with glittering tears.

Maya held the other woman's gaze, her dark eyes filling as well. Sadness and yearning emanated from the teen.

Then Katerina took a step forward. "Oh, my beautiful girl!"

As Katerina Franco wrapped her arms around Maya Velasquez, for several anxious seconds Sam feared that Jade's mother believed that her daughter was not dead after all. But then Katerina moved her hands to Maya's shoulders and leaned back, gazing intently at the teen's face as she murmured, "Welcome, Maya."

The normally stoic girl burst into tears. Digging through her purse, Maya extracted the two tiny figurines that had graced Jade's desk in the dorm room. Sniffling, she held them out to Katerina. "These seemed important, so I brought them for you."

"They're yours." Pushing the pronghorn and javelina carvings back toward Maya, Katerina embraced the girl again, holding her longer this time. "I'm happy to know you exist, sweetheart."

# 24

Sam left Maya with Jade's mother, promising to buy the girl a plane ticket back to Bellingham whenever Maya was ready to leave, then Sam drove back from Santa Fe to the research station the next day. After sunset, when she was at her desk in her dorm room working on her articles, she heard the window rattle and turned to witness a long snout poking in through the dislodged screen. Sam froze in her chair to watch. The coati soon managed to thrust its entire head through the opening, then, with a wriggle, dropped through the opening onto Jade's desk.

Spotting Sam on the other side of the room, the creature paused, one paw in the air, its white-ringed eyes huge in the dimly lit room.

"I was hoping you'd come back, coati-friend," Sam told her. "I've got something for you."

The creature made raccoon-like chittering sounds, halfway between grunts and chirps, watching nervously as Sam slowly backed across the room to her closet area, then knelt and pulled some purple grapes out of her snack bin. When she looked up again, the coati had moved back toward the open window.

"Oh, don't go! Look what I've got for you." Sam held out the grapes, letting them dangle from her hand.

The coati swiveled to face her again, stood up on its hind legs and pressed its forepaws to its chest, flicking its nose up and snuffling all the while. It curled its long fuzzy tail around its hind quarters, torn between the desire to possess those grapes and the urge to flee.

The grapes won out. The creature sat as Sam slowly approached, holding the grapes out at arm's length. When the fruit was close enough, the coati quickly grabbed at them with its front paws. Sam held tight to the stem, not wanting the creature to vanish through the window with the whole bunch. She slowly edged onto Jade's bed, and watched the coati pull off one grape at a time.

"I was going to call you Jade," she whispered. "But that hurts too much, so maybe Luisa? That was her middle name."

The coati was much more interested in the next bite than in whatever Sam decided to name it. It munched each grape quickly, making smacking noises now, its nose quivering and its eyes warily watching her every move.

"Or maybe you're a boy? If that's true, you could be Luis."

Both Sam and the coati startled when the door opened on the other side of the room. Chase stepped in and set a suitcase down at his feet. The coati fled to the window frame, but stopped there, chittering and sniffling loudly, its long snout jerking up and down.

"Chase!" Sam exclaimed. "I wasn't expecting you."

"What," he gestured to the animal sitting on the window sill, "is *that*?"

"That's Luisa. At least, I think she's a female. She's a coatimundi. They mostly live in Central America. This is the extreme northern end of their range, so I'm really lucky to see one here."

Chase stayed next to the door. "It came in through the window?"

"This is the second time. I was hoping she'd come back." She held the grapes out closer to the coati, and the creature turned to eat again.

"Why am I not surprised?" Chase said. "Jaguars and trogons and elf owls . . . Do those things get rabies?"

Sam chuckled at the scene: a coati on one side of the room and her lover on the other, and both looking ready to flee any second. "She's like a tropical raccoon, Chase. She's harmless."

He took a step farther into the room. "Raccoons are never harmless. You've seen what they did to my cabin."

"True," she had to admit. The masked bandits had nested in his attic and shredded the insulation there. "But they are cute. And this one's, well, exotic, don't you think? I've never seen a wild coati before."

Chase took two more steps into the room. Luisa yanked the last grape from the stalk, stuffed it into her mouth, and zipped out the window.

Sam stood up. Chase quickly crossed the room and slid the window shut before he turned to embrace her.

"I thought you were staying in Las Vegas," she murmured after they'd kissed. "But I'm glad you're here."

"The lab recovered some photos from Jade's camera," he told her. "They're not what we hoped for. They're blurred; nothing recognizable. But I wanted you to see them anyway."

She was amazed he'd driven all that way just to bring her blurry photos. "You could have emailed them to me."

Chase shook his head. "Security issues; they need to stay on my phone." He kissed her again. "Probably another dead end. I wanted to cushion that blow if I could."

She pulled away. "You can cushion me later. Show me those photos."

They both sat on Jade's bed as Chase pulled out his cell phone and scrolled to the photos sent from the FBI lab. He handed the phone to Sam.

The first image was nearly black, like the photo of the jaguar Jade had sent her. "I want this." She waved the phone at him. "I might be able to rescue it with Photoshop."

When he didn't respond, she thumbed to the next. A fuzzy brown photo—maybe of the ground. She'd taken a few like that herself, unintentionally pressing a button while holding her cell phone.

The next was also blurred, as Chase had said, but at least it had some color. The dirt color, again, but in the corner, a splash of blue-green cut by a gray undulating shape like an elongated backward *S*. Sam studied it, squinting, trying to bring the image into focus. Somehow it seemed familiar, but her brain couldn't place it.

"Damn it," she muttered.

"I know." Chase patted her thigh. "They're disappointing."

"Can you give me copies of these?"

"No. Like I said, security issues. They were labeled 'law enforcement eyes only.'"

She scowled at him.

"Sorry. Maybe someone in the sheriff's office can decipher something," he answered mildly. "We shared these photos with them."

"Okay." She chewed her lower lip in frustration, disappointed in her inability to recognize a clue in the photos.

"Do you have any of that tequila?" Chase asked.

"That was Adam's gift. He got it from the women next door."

Chase frowned at the mention of the reporter. "Thank God the rock star's gone."

The "rock star" hadn't gone far, but Chase didn't need to know that. Sam knew Adam was in Tucson, still snooping around for details to wrap up his Arizona reportage with a big red sensational bow.

"I have merlot," she offered.

"Now you're talking. Back in a minute." He stood up and slipped out the door, no doubt headed to the men's room across the courtyard.

Sam picked up his phone. The greenish photo was still on the screen. She couldn't see any way to send it to herself. Damn. She wanted to study those blurs, maybe work on them with Photoshop.

Spinning, she grabbed up her own phone, switched into camera mode, and took a photo of Chase's cell phone screen. Swiping back through the previous two images, she took photos of those as well. When she heard a hand on the door knob, she dropped his cell back onto the bed where he'd left it.

Chase gazed at her expectantly.

Looking down, she quickly punched the Gallery icon on her phone and switched to her stored photos. "I wanted to show you the pictures I took of Jade's shrine at the wall." Swiping to the first, she held out the phone.

"No need," Chase said. "I saw Steele's tear-jerk 'special report.'" He put the last two words in air quotes. "Where's that wine? I hoped you would have poured me a glass by the time I got back."

# 25

Why would the cartel dress Jade in an old, stained men's shirt? Jade normally dressed in shirts that were tailored to her attractive figure. Was putting her in a man's shirt a jab at the fact that she was bisexual? Sam couldn't see the point.

And why take off Imhoff's uniform shirt and leave his equipment in his SUV? And then dump both their bodies in the desert? Clearly, the killers wanted Jade and Imhoff to remain unidentified, lost among all the anonymous dead in the southwest desert. Was that supposed to send a message that they were trash, like the undocumented migrants? In Jade's case, the Patriot Posse seemed like potential suspects for that sort of behavior, but she couldn't see the foursome doing that to a border patrol agent.

Was the green plaid she'd seen in the shed with the rattlesnake Jade's shirt? Was Imhoff's in there as well? Could their clothing help identify the killers in any way? Sam's thoughts swirled all night.

In the morning, she told Chase about the shed and the green plaid shirt.

He raised an eyebrow. "Something else you forgot to tell me."

"I didn't think it was important. It didn't lead me any closer to Jade. And there was a humongous rattler."

"Uh-huh," Chase muttered, distracted by catching the corner of his toothpaste tube in the zipper of his travel kit.

"I should go back there, see for sure if it's hers."

He put his hands on her shoulders. "*Querida*, just call the sheriff's office. Then you'll have done your duty. Whatever they choose to do with that information is their business."

Sam was nearly certain they'd choose to do nothing. Their cartel theory would go down in the Silva and Imhoff case files as the solution to the murders. Done. Nobody messed with the cartels and lived to tell about it.

Chase bent down for a kiss. "I'll see you at home in ten days, right?"

"More like thirteen, since I'm driving," she said. "I'll bring Luisa back with me if I can find a carrier."

"Luisa?"

"The coati. After I've trained her a little. She needs to learn how to use a litter box if I'm going to keep her in the house. Or maybe she could stay at your cabin?"

Chase gazed uncertainly at her.

"I'm kidding, Chase."

"Thank God."

As soon as Chase had left, Sam copied the blurry photos to her laptop and opened them in Photoshop. She tried lightening the images, increasing the contrast, changing them to shades of gray and sepia. Nothing made any shape clearer. It was obvious the photos had been snapped while the camera was in motion, and the horrific image of her friend being shot and falling to the ground with cell phone in hand kept replaying in Sam's mind.

The green blur continued to haunt her. That smeary gray backward *S*. It reminded her a bit of Frannie Straub's painting, like an abstract of a waterfall snaking down a cliff.

But if her memory served her, the colors of Frannie's

painting didn't match these.

Groaning in frustration, she reverted back to the original photos and reported to the dining hall for her lunch duties.

Sam had no intention of leaving this area until Jade's killer was identified. She probably knew more about Jade's last days than anyone else right now. And she definitely cared more than anyone else.

The man's T-shirt. The green blur. Imhoff. The shed. How did any of it fit together? Had Jade and Imhoff been caught by a jealous lover in some sort of hot-sex rendezvous in the shed? Ugh. Sam couldn't imagine that anyone would choose such an ugly place to meet. Plus, Jade didn't have a lover, at least not one she'd talked about, and Naomi didn't seem like she would waddle through the desert to shoot her fiancé. And how had Jade's CR-V and Imhoff's patrol vehicle ended up where they did? Nothing made sense.

As she wiped down tables in the dining hall, Sam decided to focus on one thing at a time. In the coroner's photo, the man's T-shirt that Jade wore had looked like a throwaway. Who would have an old T-shirt at hand to dress a body in? Hell, as sweaty and dusty as this part of the world was, every man would. She'd seen bags of T-shirt rags in the Straubs' entryway and in Dulcie Thorensen's trunk. RTK Construction probably used them to clean equipment, wipe dust from all those white trucks.

Sam's imagination snagged on RTK. All those beefy men in sweaty shirts. The owners had been so defensive at her insinuation that they might employ illegal migrants. Had Jade stumbled onto some secret of theirs, maybe seen illegals sneaking into their staff dormitory quarters? But Imhoff didn't fit into that scenario.

The partners had even offered her a job at RTK, for heaven's sake. And Dulcie had seemed so sympathetic, both in the office and at the wall. Although showing Sam photos of her children seemed like an odd thing to do at a shrine to a murdered girl.

A memory suddenly struck her: Dulcie's car was green. The same shade of green as the blurry image captured on Jade's phone?

She returned to her room and brought up the green blur again. A metallic bluish-green. It could be a car finish. A photo caught in motion was usually elongated, right? Using Photoshop, Sam squished the photo horizontally. No help. But compressing the image vertically—the backward *S* now looked more like a *Z*. The Z-shaped scrape on the green Audi's bumper?

Sam sat back in her chair, fixated on the image. Was she hallucinating? Dulcie? Why would Jade have a photo of the Thorensens' car?

Dulcie's reaction to Jade's photo in the company lunch room had seemed so compassionate. As had her tears at the wall. Sam swallowed. She had categorized Dulcie Thorensen as a kind-hearted soul, like that server in Bisbee. Had Dulcie's gestures of sympathy actually been signs of guilt?

There had been rags in the Audi's trunk. There were three grown males in the Thorensen house; there'd be plenty of old stained T-shirts. Shit! Dulcie?

There was no way one woman could pull off the two murders and dispose of the bodies on her own. Then someone had to drive Jade's CR-V to Tombstone, and Imhoff's duty vehicle back to Douglas. And then the driver would need a ride back to his or her own vehicle.

There were two Thorensens. And a whole host of loyal employees. But it would be risky to involve any of the RTK workers, wouldn't it? Where did the Thorensens live? She looked up the business records for RTK. No help there; only the address of the headquarters was listed. But Cochise County property records showed that Philip and Dulcina Thorensen lived in Douglas. One of them could have returned Imhoff's SUV to the grocery store's parking lot in the dark, couldn't they?

Sam looked at the computer screen. Nobody was going to take her seriously, agree that this squished green blur matched the Audi's bumper. She'd manipulated the photo, and the colors still seemed off.

She copied the altered photo to her phone and stuffed a baseball cap and a bottle of water into her daypack. On her way to her car, she stopped at the office and told the director that she would be gone for the rest of the day.

It took her a little more than an hour to find the shrine again. Some of the cards had been blown away from the wall, and a few were branded with tire tracks. Using a tissue, she retrieved them, and after looking at them, returned them to the drift of items left along the base of the wall. After picking up several cards, she finally located Dulcie's. The inside held only a handwritten message: "Praying for you. –RTK Construction." The words seemed more like an ad than a message of sympathy or expression of loss.

Wrapping the card in another tissue, Sam went back to her car and drove to the Cochise County Sheriff's Office in Bisbee.

A young male deputy manned the front desk. When he spotted her, he said, "How can I help you, Miz Westin?"

Sam paused, startled. "Have we met, Deputy"—she read his name tag—"Layh?"

"Haven't had the pleasure," he drawled, his eyebrows knitted together in a frown. "But I saw you on the news. That report where you complained we weren't doing our jobs?"

*Shit.* The first report, the one where Adam had focused the camera on her.

"I'd like to speak to Deputy Ortega," she told him.

"Well, that's tough," he responded. "Because this is her day off. Looks like you'll have to give me your complaint this time."

Sam hesitated, a string of curse words running a tickertape through her head. "It'll wait." She turned back to the door.

"Have a nice day!" he called after her.

In her car, Sam used her cell phone to look up property ownership records again, praying that D. Ortega was not a renter. There were several Ortegas, but only one *D*, so she was betting that J.M. and D.C. Ortega lived at the address shown in Bisbee.

The house was modest, but newer and rectangular, not wrapped around a cliff or squeezed between boulders like so many of the older homes in the town. The deputy answered the door, dressed in shorts and a T-shirt, her dark hair caught back in a ponytail. As she pushed open the screen door, her brown eyes showed suspicion. "Miss Westin. What are you doing here?"

"The cartel didn't kill Jade and Imhoff," Sam blurted. "You need to check out the Thorensens."

Ortega studied Sam's face for several seconds. Finally, she pushed the door open wider. "You'd better come in."

# 26

"We arrested both the Thorensens this morning before they left the house," a smiling Deputy Ortega told Sam the next afternoon at the sheriff's office in Bisbee. "You were right; it looks like the shirt Silva was dressed in came from the rag pile in the trunk of their Audi. And you were also right about the photo matching the car bumper. We found Imhoff's uniform shirt and Silva's blouse in that shed you mentioned, although the earring you picked up doesn't match anyone that we know of. But most important, the marks on the bullets retrieved from their bodies match the rifle owned by Phil Thorensen."

Sam nodded. "Good."

"Thank you for bringing me that card. We recovered a fingerprint from Dulcie Thorensen that matches prints in the vehicles, and the tear stain may provide DNA that will match traces in one or both vehicles; we won't know that for a while."

If she hadn't been so depressed by the tragedy, Sam might have cheered.

"We're holding them in separate cells, of course," Ortega said. "The husband isn't cooperating, but Mrs. Thorensen's singing like a parakeet. I've got to go back in now." She nodded toward a room with an unmarked door. "Deputy Layh, please allow Miss Westin to watch the video feed."

Frowning slightly at Ortega, he said, "I thought today was your day off."

She stuck her tongue out at him. "Jealous, Mike? This was worth coming in for."

A disgruntled Deputy Layh accompanied Sam into the observation room and silently pulled up a chair by her side.

On the video monitor, Dulcie Thorensen hunched over a table in the interview room, sobbing uncontrollably into her hands. Ortega sat down across from her on the other side of the table and spoke aloud for the microphone, stating her presence and Dulcie's, then said, "Interview continuing, 1:32 p.m."

Ortega then simply watched Dulcie for several moments that seemed to stretch into hours. Finally, Dulcie's demeanor changed. Lifting her head, she pushed her hair out of her eyes, and abruptly stated, "It wasn't me."

"What do you mean by that?" Ortega asked. "You were there."

"My husband and I were both there. We were driving to Naco for a meeting with Xtel Instruments—"

"Xtel?" Ortega interrupted.

Dulcie waved an impatient hand in the air. "They're headquartered in Tucson, but we were supposed to meet in Naco. They make sensors and security cameras and such. But Phil wanted to check some work on the goddamned wall so we were driving along the border road. It wasn't even dawn yet. He wanted to get there before his crew did."

Ortega made a note on her pad.

"I was in the passenger seat with my eyes closed, trying to catch up on my beauty sleep, but then Phil woke me up, yelling 'Goddamn it!' And I looked, and I saw that jaguar. I couldn't believe it. A jaguar, right there, practically beneath our name on the fence!"

She took a sip of water from the glass on the table. "I didn't see why Phil was so upset. He stomped on the brake so hard it nearly gave me whiplash, then he jumped out and got his rifle from the trunk. But the jaguar took off before he could aim." Dulcie swallowed hard, her eyes focused on her hands, now clasped together on top of the table.

"And then," Ortega prompted.

"And then that girl stood up, and she had her cell phone in her hand, and she'd obviously been taking a photo of the jaguar." Dulcie drew in a big breath, then exhaled slowly. "And that's when Phil really got mad, yelling at her to give him that phone. She ran to her car and drove off down the access road and then Phil took off right after her."

So the Audi had been the car enveloped in dust in Maria's video clip.

Dulcie stopped for a moment, covered her eyes, then swiped tears to the sides, streaking mascara back onto her temples before she dropped her hands again. "He only tapped her back bumper with the front bumper of the Audi, I swear, but she fishtailed in the gravel, then she jumped out and ran partway into the bushes. And Phil was yelling at her about the camera and he only fired a shot over her head, and she tripped and fell onto her hands and knees."

Dulcie inhaled another deep breath, but it sounded more like a gasp as her eyes filled with tears again. "And it all would have still been all right, you know, if only she'd given Phil that goddamn phone!"

Ortega nudged a box of tissues closer to Dulcie, and the other woman pulled out one to wipe her eyes.

Sam's heart pounded in her chest. Jade must have been terrified. But Sam knew her friend would also have been defiant. Anyone who would face poachers in Zimbabwe would certainly not have backed down to a pair of angry middle-aged Americans.

"But ..." Ortega drew out the word, urging Dulcie to continue.

"But she wouldn't. She picked that phone up out of the dirt and actually aimed it at us." Dulcie's throat flexed as she swallowed. "And that's when Phil just lost it."

"How did he 'lose it'?" Ortega queried.

Dulcie thrust both hands out to her sides. "He shot her. Twice! I couldn't—" She paused, put her hands over her eyes again. "I couldn't ... believe ... he did that."

"Why did your husband shoot Jade Silva?"

Dulcie lowered her hands. "That damn jaguar! You live here; you remember how crazy people got when someone took a photo of a jaguar in Arizona a couple of years ago."

"That was pretty special," Ortega commented.

"*Special?*" Dulcie's voice rose an octave. "It's just another predator that would kill cattle and horses and even people. Worse than those goddamned wolves outsiders keep bringing in." She leaned forward. "And then, remember all that trouble with that photo of the javelinas at the wall?"

Ortega nodded, sounding sympathetic now. "The sow and five piglets, looking for a way through."

"Omigod, remember the protests down at the wall?" Dulcie actually rolled her eyes. "They even threatened to tear it down. We couldn't work there for weeks until those environuts finally went home. Can you imagine what would happen if that photo of a jaguar got around? And that section has our name on it! That girl was threatening our whole business!" Dulcie shook her head, intent on a self-righteous-justification roll now. "Think of all the jobs we created. Shooting that girl was self-defense, if you think about it."

"And Agent Imhoff?"

"Oh!" Dulcie's brash manner abruptly crumpled, and she was back to tears again. "That, that border patrol car drove up and that man, that agent, got out," she stuttered. "He had his hand on his weapon and he was screaming at Phil to drop the rifle, and then . . . oh God, Phil shot him, too."

Dulcie dissolved into hysterical sobs, throwing her arms down onto the table and lowering her face on top of them. Ortega glanced once at the camera, then sat quietly and watched the woman cry for a few minutes before she asked, "Do you need a break, Mrs. Thorensen?"

After a few more seconds, the sobs diminished, and Dulcie again raised her blotchy face. After wiping her face with a tissue and taking several shuddering breaths, she said, "A break? No, I don't need a *break*. I need to go home."

"You can have a fifteen-minute break," Ortega offered.

Dulcie put both hands on the table and leaned forward. "Like I just told you, it wasn't me. Phil shot them both."

"But you helped him load their bodies into the CR-V, didn't you? And you left the bodies in the desert, taking their clothes to make it look like they were migrants, and you drove Jade's car to where it was abandoned, didn't you? And then Phil drove you back to the kill site and you drove Imhoff's patrol car to Douglas while Phil went back to work, didn't you? How did you get home from the grocery-store lot, Mrs. Thorensen?"

"Good question," Deputy Layh muttered at Sam's side.

"Lyft? Uber?" Sam quietly suggested.

Layh shot her an irritated look but pulled a sheet from the notepad on the desk and scribbled a note, which he folded and stuck into his shirt pocket.

On the monitor, Dulcie locked eyes with Deputy Ortega for a long, tense moment. Then she finally said, "I want a lawyer."

"Didn't you do all that?" Ortega reiterated. "We have your

fingerprints on both the CR-V and the border patrol vehicle steering wheels. We also have your DNA."

Dulcie slapped both hands down on the table. "Lawyer! I want a lawyer!"

"Interview concluded, 2:05 p.m.," Ortega said aloud for the microphone.

The deputy at Sam's side switched off the monitor, and Sam stood up, her emotions swirling, so hotly intense that she felt dizzy. When her other friends had died, it had been for reasons that were horrific, but at least more easily justified. But this! This was only about money. How many people had trashed their entire code of morality over that border wall?

When Deputy Ortega emerged into the room after locking Dulcie in her cell, Sam thanked her for allowing her to watch the interview.

"I won't share a word with anyone," Sam promised. "Not with Adam Steele. Not even with my significant other, FBI Agent Chase Perez. You pursued the leads."

"Most of which were provided by you. Thanks for all your help."

Sam nodded. "Your office can choose what they want to share."

Ortega smiled. "Feel free to tell that gorgeous Adam Steele that we've arrested the Thorensens for the murders of Silva and Imhoff."

"Then I can guarantee that you'll see him later today. He'll be thrilled."

"I'll warn my boss. And I'll be sure to comb my hair and put on some lipstick, too." Ortega chuckled, then her expression sobered. "We may be in touch as the trial approaches."

"I'll probably be back in Washington State by then, Deputy Ortega."

"Daniela," the deputy offered, holding out her hand. "Thank you."

"You have all my contact information." Sam shook her hand.

After exiting through the front door of the station, Sam sat for a moment on the bench out front in the shade of a tree. She called Adam's cell phone, left the message on his voice mail. Then she closed her eyes, trying to cool her anger enough to drive.

Money, money, money. Two million dollars per mile of wall. She envisioned the Thorensens crushed under all that steel and concrete, under all the surveillance cameras and trucks and cranes and guns they supplied for the project. She threw Ramirez and Kidd under that pile, too, for good measure. And then, she added the human traffickers and drug smugglers.

Finally, she added all the employers who profited from hiring the undocumented migrants pouring into the country and wanted to keep them forever in the shadows. She'd never heard a word on the news about including *them* in any raid. The spineless politicians who worked for lobbyists instead of the common good belonged in that crush pile, too.

All the desperation, all the violence, all the destruction—it was all about money.

Gradually, the tension drained away and Sam became aware of the breeze cooling her sweating forehead, of the leaves fluttering in the tree overhead and the birds twittering in its branches. Unclenching her fists, she took a deep breath and let her thoughts drift to happier moments here in Arizona. To the funny snuffling sounds made by Luisa, the nose-twitching coatimundi, to the flashes of purple, green, black, and scarlet feathers from a dozen species of hummingbirds, to the tiny, slit-eyed owls in the cavity nests of the sycamores and the elegant trogons perched on the white branches.

Her brain drifted to the Broads and the researchers at the station, with their passion for nature and wild creatures, and to fellow wildlife biologist Diego Xintal. Some humans were worth saving.

Finally, her thoughts circled back to the best of all. El Guapo, the jaguar. The intense beauty of his green eyes, the unique ebony rosette patterns scattered artistically across his ochre fur. The haughtiness of the jaguar's gaze. The awe-inspiring moments of simply sharing the world with such a magnificent wild animal.

Then her brain returned to the photo that started it all. The way the big cat's desperation at the wall had been revealed when she lightened Jade's photo.

And Sam finally understood how this chapter of her life had to end.

# 27

The flames of the blowtorches were so bright that Sam feared they could be seen for miles. Even with two, it seemed to take forever to cut through the metal mesh. "Hurry," she hissed. "We've only got minutes."

Diego Xintal answered over his shoulder, his voice muffled by the hooded black sweatshirt he wore and the kerchief over his mouth. "I'm nearly done."

"Me too," Chase mumbled through his own kerchief.

On this night, when they could have used some background noise for cover, the wind had chosen not to blow and the wall stood in ominous silence. With a clatter that was much too loud, the square of metal wall mesh fell to the ground on the Mexican side. Both men tossed their blowtorches into the darkness behind them.

The first masked figure quickly climbed through the opening. Sam followed, snagging her overlarge sweatshirt on the ragged edges of the mesh. Then Maya wriggled her way to the other side.

"Handing him through," Xintal hissed, then he and Chase pushed the heavy cage through the hole before they, too, crossed over.

Headlights flashed over a hill in the distance. "Quick!" Sam urged, grabbing the hand of the last figure, the cameraman, pulling him through the hole.

Adam laughed as he tripped over the mesh square lying at his feet. "Got it! This is priceless!"

The headlights bounced over the next hill, nearing.

"Grab the cage and run!" Xintal urged.

All six of them slid their gloved fingers through the bars of the cage and lifted the heavy jaguar. After treeing El Guapo using Xintal's friend's trained hunting dogs, they'd tranquilized him with a dart, and stuffed the cat into the smallest cage he'd fit into. The jaguar growled now as he was rocked from one side of the cage to another, but he stayed inert as his carriers jogged into the thick brush. They resorted to dragging the cage through the bushes as they dove to their bellies to hide among the shrubbery. Sam prayed the sedative would hold for at least another hour.

They crouched low among the bushes as lights strobed above them.

Katerina Franco whispered, "They won't shoot, will they?"

"I hope not," Xintal responded.

"It's not their jurisdiction," Chase pointed out. "We just broke out of the US and invaded Mexico. I don't think border patrol would like to advertise that."

"I love it!" Adam chuckled. "The networks will love it, too!" He tapped Sam on the shoulder. "Maybe we could get a documentary out of it, too, babe."

"Don't call me babe," she told him for the fortieth time.

"I can't believe I'm doing this," Maya said. "This is so sweet!"

Sam could hardly believe it herself, and she'd organized the whole escapade. She patted her back pocket to make sure her passport was still there and wondered what US authorities would think when there was no record of her entry to Mexico. Chase assured her that they were unlikely to check, and if they did, he'd say the Mexicans simply hadn't recorded their entry. It was in vogue right now to blame Mexico for pretty much everything.

After ten minutes of lights flashing overhead and the distant sound of radio chatter from the other side of the wall, the border patrol moved away. The jaguar rescue team waited as the sounds faded, making sure they'd gone.

Abruptly, they heard the sound of breaking brush and muffled thuds of footsteps coming their way.

"*Carajo! Federales*?" Chase asked Xintal.

"Relax." Xintal pushed back his hood. "My guys."

Four muscular young Mexican men carried the jaguar cage to a waiting pickup, and they all piled in. Adam and his camera took the front passenger seat, Katerina squeezed into the back seat with two of the Mexicans as the third drove over the rough ground, headlights off. In the truck bed, Sam crouched between Chase and the fourth Mexican on one side of the cage, and Maya and Diego Xintal bumped shoulders on the other.

Sam touched Chase's bare forearm. "Thank you for this."

"I was never here," he retorted, his teeth gleaming white in the dim starlight. "I'm on vacation in Hermosillo, Mexico." His grin told her Chase was actually enjoying this escapade.

"I'm there, too," she said.

"I can't remember any of your names," Diego Xintal stated in a sober voice. "And you don't look like anyone I recognize, either."

"Ditto," Maya whispered.

Inside the cage, the jaguar twitched a couple of times.

Sam warned Xintal, "He's waking up."

"We're almost there," he responded.

The pickup rocked to a stop amid a small grove of palo verde trees. The ten people climbed out, and the four young

Mexicans moved the cage from the pickup bed to the ground in front of the truck, speaking in rapid Spanish.

"We're on the northern border of the jaguar preserve," Chase translated for Sam.

Inside the cage, Sam saw the jaguar's eyes were open. Taking a last chance to savor the moment, she thrust her fingers through the mesh of the cage to touch that magnificent fur. The big cat twisted its head to glare at her. El Guapo's expression seemed serene, but that was probably the tranquilizer's effect. In the dim light, the jaguar's eyes were a beautiful jade green.

*Jade.* The word slipped from her brain and snagged on her heart. Sam felt her roommate's presence as if Jade Silva were standing close by in the darkness.

Stroking an index finger over the jaguar's velvety fur, she murmured in a low voice, "I apologize to your kind on behalf of my species. If I could make the insanity stop, I would."

Behind her, Maya whispered, "Amen."

Xintal flashed a penlight into El Guapo's eyes. The jaguar hissed and turned his head away from the light. Xintal passed the penlight to Sam and then pulled a syringe from his pocket. Holding it up in the small circle of brightness, he pushed the plunger until liquid spilled from its needle.

Maya gasped.

"Antidote," Xintal explained. "We can't set him free if he's too groggy."

Reaching through the mesh, he jabbed El Guapo in the hindquarters. The jaguar spat and nearly flipped the small cage as he tried to turn and grab his attacker.

"I guess that means he's ready," Chase noted dryly.

Xintal moved toward the cage door.

"Wait!" Adam positioned himself at an angle to the cage, camera in hand. "Ready for lights?"

Xintal, Katerina, Sam, and Maya pulled up their hoods and bandanas. Chase moved back into the shadows, completely out of camera range.

At Adam's signal, one of the Mexicans switched on the truck's headlights, spotlighting the cage. And then all four Mexicans proudly took positions in the light close to the cage.

Xintal pulled the door open and then stood back.

El Guapo stared straight ahead, into the dark brush beyond the light. After a quick glance at the surrounding humans, the jaguar raised his chin toward the mountains in the distance. His mouth opened briefly as he scented the air. Then he abruptly shot out of the cage, vanishing into the night in a fraction of a second.

They all cheered. Sam held up a hand, her fingers separated in a very old gesture. "Live long and prosper, Guapo."

Even the Mexicans knew the old Star Trek tribute. "Live long an' prosper!" they echoed, copying the gesture.

"*Que viva el tigre*," one murmured, his hushed voice sounding like a prayer.

"*Viva!*" repeated nearly everyone.

Sam glanced at Adam. They were the only two non-Spanish speakers. Here in Mexico, they were the outsiders. She couldn't be sure in the dark, but she thought Adam winked back at her.

Katerina wrapped an arm around Maya. "I think Jade would be proud."

Sam knew her young friend was smiling by the lilt in Maya's voice as she answered, "I *know* she would be."

"And that's a wrap," Adam pronounced. The lights snapped off.

Sam felt Chase approaching, then his fingers intertwined with hers.

For a long moment, all ten humans stood without speaking or moving, savoring the tranquility of the dark night, the magnificent vastness of the galaxies shining overhead, and the sounds of the wilderness that surrounded them.

If you enjoyed BORDERLAND,
please recommend it to another reader
or consider writing a review on any online site.
Recommendations and reviews
help authors get the word out about their books.
Thank you!

The following is an excerpt from the beginning of
*Race with Danger*, the first book in my Run for Your Life
adventure/suspense trilogy.

# Race with Danger
## Prologue

It wasn't even eleven p.m. How could the streets of Bellingham be so deserted? There wasn't a person, or even a cat, in sight. Most of the house windows were black. Was any door safe to pound on? I felt like screaming, but I barely had enough breath to run. Even if I'd had the extra air or seconds to spare, I couldn't afford to call attention to myself.

I was supposed to be in my bedroom studying that night. Instead, I'd answered my friends' texts and joined them on an expedition through the vast Bayview graveyard. It was the night before Halloween and it was appropriately uber-creepy dark. Cold thick clouds smothered the moon and stars. We headed for our favorite side-by-side headstones, so old their edges were rounded and so furry with moss that nobody could make out the names underneath, if names were ever there at all. We each had our stories for them. Mine was about star-crossed lovers. The man had been drafted during World War II, and although his girlfriend was terrified that he'd be shredded by bullets in Europe or come home with only one leg, she—of course—vowed to wait forever for him.

Here's the twist: despite several close calls, he made it home in one piece, carrying an excellent antique engagement ring given to him by a grateful Jewish widow he saved in France. But once he was back in Bellingham, he found out that his girlfriend died two months before in an explosion in the munitions factory where she worked. He couldn't live without her, so he drank poison while kneeling on her grave so they would get to spend eternity together. I liked to think they even had little ghost children that came up from the ground to play tag among the graves on foggy nights.

Of course, that night being so close to Halloween, we went beyond our usual romantic ghost tales and told stories of vampires and axe murderers and zombies. When the breeze whipped a whirlwind of black leaves up in front of us, we all streaked away in different directions, shrieking. After we found each other again in the dark, we laughed it off. But when sleet started to ping off our windbreakers, we headed home to our books and beds.

That's when my real nightmare started.

It was a lot more difficult to fish-flop in through my bedroom window than it was to slither out, so I peeked through our living room window to see if it was safe to sneak through the front door. The lamps had been turned off inside, which usually meant that my parents had gone to bed. From the living room I could see through into the kitchen, and the light was on over the stove.

My dad was a late-night snacker, so I stood there for a minute to make sure he didn't appear at the refrigerator door. After a few seconds of studying the shadows, my eyes sorted out some unusual shapes on the living room floor. At first I thought one might be Joker, our black Lab, but the shapes weren't really the same dense black that he was. It took a few minutes more before my brain identified what I was staring at.

My parents lay on the ivory carpet, their arms and legs kinked at odd angles, as if they were trying to swim through the dark pools of blood surrounding them.

For a while, I couldn't tear my gaze away, because that couldn't be real, could it? Was it some sort of pre-Halloween joke? Yeah, they'd done plenty of embarrassing things in the past, like putting a *Lawn Care by Amelia* sign out for all the neighbors to see when I didn't mow the lawn. But would they go to this extreme to punish me for sneaking out?

Then I heard my little brother scream, and two men dragged Aaron out of the hallway in his pajamas. The men were dressed like ninjas, all in black, and they wore ski masks that erased their features. One ninja stepped into the pool of light in the kitchen. His ski mask reduced his face to two eyeholes and a pair of oval lips. Between the bottom edge of his mask and the collar of his black shirt were two curved V shapes like flying birds.

He turned in my direction, and between Aaron's shrieks, I heard him hiss out a word as he pointed to me. "There!"

I knew I had to run for my life. I was a few yards from the street corner when a car engine started up behind me, but I didn't look back. I raced down the next street. It was still sleeting, and the ice pellets and wind were slapping down wet cold leaves from the trees overhead. I took shortcuts between houses and zigged and zagged until I didn't even know where I was.

I careened down the street between parked cars and hurtled over a kid's skateboard, trying to stick to the shadows of limbs overhanging the sidewalk. Headlights swung around the corner behind me. I slipped on a drift of wet leaves and almost crashed down on one knee, jamming my wrist as I saved myself from a full face-plant with one hand to the concrete. As I pushed myself back to my feet, the high beams hit me full force in the back. The engine revved louder behind me. The tires squealed on the wet pavement as the car closed in. Its headlights flared around my shadow to illuminate a solid wall at the end of a cul-de-sac—a privacy fence at least six feet tall.

What choice did I have? I leapt.

My ribs landed hard against the top edge. I jackknifed over into the blackness. As my running shoes hit the ground, I heard the growl of an animal that was big and heavy. And mad.

Maybe that dog was chained or maybe it was only slow because I'd surprised it from a deep sleep. But I made it to the other side of the yard before it did.

That's how I found out I was a runner.

I've been running ever since.

# One

## Three Years Later

"Zany Grey," the loudspeaker announces. For some reason, the voice or maybe the name encourages a big red parrot to squawk from the palm tree overhead, like he's adding a verbal exclamation point.

I flinch inwardly at that name like I always do, but then I slap on my happy face and step forward, emerging from beneath the gigantic red-and-white banner that reads *Verde Island Endurance Team Competition*. It seems weird that the race colors are red and white, since *verde* means green, but maybe the organizers don't know Spanish.

*Zany.* I hate how everyone thinks it's cute to make up nicknames for athletes. When I picked my new name, I was aiming for Tana for short. That's what my friends call me. I expected Tanya and Tanz and maybe even Tanza, but Zany?

And then, to make it even worse, certain newsquackers

keep referring to me as 'The African American Princess of Endurance Racing,' which is beyond annoying, like all human beings need to be labeled and categorized. Only the mentally-challenged care about that skin-color sort of race anymore.

And yeah, by now I've also heard about the geezer who wrote cowboy books—Zane Grey. Moldy old history. Nobody I hang with ever heard of that Grey, and besides, like I just mentioned, *I* didn't choose that stupid name Zany.

I gave myself the name Tanzania to honor my mother. She was raised in Africa, although to set the record straight, she grew up in Zimbabwe, not Tanzania. My father came from Chicago. They met when he was on some sort of business trip in Africa. But none of my fans has discovered those details. As far as they know, my parents died tragically nearly a decade ago. I reversed Mom and Dad's skin colors, too, not only to add confusion but to emphasize the point that this country just needs to get over the whole Black and White thing. That's why I chose the last name Grey. I think the world would be a better place if everyone was a mutt like me.

The bronzed emcee is wearing a very untropical suit and a red and white tie that matches the race banner. His pancake makeup is starting to melt in the muggy heat, but his hair gel is gamely hanging in, gluing every strand into a perfect blond helmet.

"Choose your teammate." He gestures dramatically with his manicured hand toward a crystal bowl on a table in front of the cameras. I'm amazed that the intense sun blazing through the cut glass isn't burning holes in the tablecloth.

The crowd claps quietly, which is pretty much all they can do, because there aren't many of them. The people in attendance are mostly race officials, camera teams, and newsquackers. At most of my races in the States, Marisela scrapes together the money to come and cheer me on. Sometimes Emilio comes, too, if he's in country and not on duty.

I could always count on a sweet kiss on the cheek from my adopted mother and a more passionate embrace from Emilio to send me into the fray. But this race is so far away from the U.S., so far away from any civilized place, that only the families of the richest competitors can afford to come.

Madelyn Hatt's parents are here, hovering as usual, smoothing down her wiry hair or straightening her race bib, constantly touching her to demonstrate that she belongs to them. Catie Cole's father made it, too, dressed in the same colors as his daughter to show they're a team. He's her manager now. His clothes are designed to complement his still-sleek body and remind everyone he used to be a famous Olympic track star.

These girls not only have parents, but parents who are managers. I don't have either.

The pathetic applause dies into an embarrassed silence. When the television station plays this later, they'll fill in the sound track with more clapping, and maybe add a digital crowd, too, to make the start of the race look like a much bigger event for the folks back home.

The cameras swivel in my direction. As I approach the glittering bowl, I take a deep breath and pray for inner calm and fantastic luck. I'm not usually a team player, so this partner element makes me sweat even more than usual. But this is the biggest race of the year with a grand prize of a million dollars, and I will win this even if I have to drag my partner up every hill and through every river on this steamy tropical island.

I have to win.

A life depends on it.

I swim my hand around the giant fishbowl, trying desperately to feel magic. Maybe I should have sanded my fingertips to make them more sensitive. Please God-If-There-Is-One, give me a little zing when I touch the name of the right partner. Give me a sign.

The slips of paper, rolled into tight little cylinders and tied with red ribbons, all feel exactly the same. No zing. As the seconds tick past, the matching blond Barbie Doll attendants standing guard at each end of the table start to shoot sideways glances at me. Their camera smiles stiffen into grimaces.

*Magic, magic, magic*, I chant in my head. I finally pull one slip out and hand it to the emcee, whose features beneath his dripping makeup are so perfect and bland that he looks like he came here directly from an Intense Botox workshop.

With a practiced flourish, he unties the bow and unfurls the note. He scans it for a second. Then he faces the camera, flashes his uber-white teeth and shouts, "Sebastian Callendro!"

My heart does an immediate crash dive. It lands on the hard ground in front of my toes and shatters into a dozen pieces. I want to fall to my knees, shake my fists at the relentless sun overhead, and scream, "No fair!"

Instead, I smile and walk a few steps forward to meet my new teammate halfway. Every camera in the place focuses on us. Callendro and I shake hands as we size each other up.

Although he's thousands of miles away right now, I can

feel waves of jealousy radiating across the airwaves from Private Emilio Santos. I know he will watch this if he can. Emilio is tall, with hair like a river of ink, eyes like bittersweet chocolate, and a swagger that everyone notices even when he's standing still. His blue-black sheen of whiskers makes him look older and more dangerous than his nineteen years, and he likes that. His almost-beard is one reason I nicknamed him Shadow, and he likes that, too.

But here, on Verde Island in the blazing sunlight of early morning, nothing is shadowy. Sebastian Callendro is maybe three inches taller than I am. I'm wearing my trademark gold tee shirt with the galloping stallion logo of my sponsor, Dark Horse Networks, on the back. Callendro's blue tee has three emblems across his chest, like a row of military medals. There's a jet zooming through a circle, then a sports car logo, then what looks like a couple of crossed test tubes, maybe an insignia for one of those monster pharma companies like the one my mom worked for. No doubt there are more designs all across his back. Holy guacamole, there's even a row of logos marching down each side of his black running shorts. Does he have decals on his butt? It's the only space left.

I guess it makes sense. Now that the word is out, Sebastian Callendro has so many sponsors that all their names won't fit on his shirt. He probably flew to Verde Island on a private jet with a real bed and real food, too.

But right now, we both have identical drips of sweat streaming down our temples. Sebastian's hair is scraped back in a ponytail, like mine, but his is a rich walnut brown, while mine is ebony with only the tiniest hints of red. The skin on the back of his extended hand tends more toward the copper spectrum than my own caramel shade. His green eyes, too light under such thick black lashes, stare into my hazel ones. His gaze is laser-intense, and just a little creepy, like he's trying to see under my skin.

Of course I've seen Sebastian Callendro before, but never so close that I can count his eyebrow hairs. He's more than a year older than I am, which makes him eighteen or maybe even nineteen. Together, we make up the youngest team in this contest—could that be an advantage?

Catie Cole is the other seventeen-year-old runner. She's the favorite golden girl—literally, because she has long blond hair and that evenly sun-kissed skin that comes from a tanning bed. She has a zillion sponsors and a modeling contract. But unfortunately, she's not just a pretty face; she's six feet tall and she runs like the wind. She's real competition.

So is Madelyn Hatt. Predictably, all the reporters call her "The Mad Hatter," although "The Mean Hatter" would probably be more accurate. Madelyn has been accused, but never convicted, of dirty tricks like putting laxatives—or was it sedatives?—in her rivals' food. She just turned nineteen. Her parents made a really big deal of it, holding a pre-birthday party before the last race we were both in. They scowled at me when I refused to wear the stupid pointy hat for the camera.

Except for Marco Senai, a perpetually emaciated runner from Kenya whom I was hoping to land as my partner, I don't know much about the men in this race. Maybe my new partner can at least contribute some usable intelligence about that. And I sure as hell hope he can keep up. Sebastian Callendro often places near the top of the men's division, but he's not a champion like me.

"I hope I don't have to drag you," I whisper, too softly for the microphones to pick up.

"And I'm not carrying you," he hisses. His smile does not extend to his eyes.

The Barbie Dolls drape numbered medallions strung on red, white, and blue ribbons around our necks. We are Team Seven. Holding up our joined hands for the camera, we step forward.

Behind us, at least two men are also stepping forward. They'll be wearing identical suits and mirrored sunglasses, and they'll have communication sets on their wrists and listening devices in their ears. Their hands will hover near the pistols holstered on their belts.

I didn't feel the magic, but I definitely got zinged with my choice.

Sebastian Callendro is The President's Son.


~ END OF PREVIEW ~


*Race with Danger* is available in bookstores and online sites, along with the other two books in the *Run for Your Life* trilogy, *Race to Truth* and *Race for Justice*.

# Acknowledgments

Every author needs help to make a book the best it can be. Beta readers Cris Carl, Alison Malfatti, and Jeanine Clifford gifted me with their candid opinions on the rough draft. Critique partner Bharti Kirchner provided valuable suggestions and insights. Ultra-professional editor Karen Brown helped to finesse language, plot, and timeline, as well as correcting my typos and grammatical mistakes, and editor Virginia Herrick helped me with the book description.

Thank you to the Great Old Broads for Wilderness for organizing a "broadwalk" at the beautiful Southwestern Research Station. I learned so much there.

And last but never least, thank you to my readers for being willing to go on another adventure with Sam Westin.

Thank you all!

# Books by
# Pamela Beason

## The Sam Westin Mysteries

Endangered

Bear Bait

Undercurrents

Backcountry

Borderland

## The Neema Mysteries

The Only Witness

The Only Clue

The Only One Left

## Romantic Suspense

Shaken

Again

Call of the Jaguar

## The Run for Your Life Adventure Trilogy

Race with Danger

Race to Truth

Race for Justice

## Nonfiction E-books

So You Want to Be a PI?

Traditional vs Indie Publishing: What to Expect

Save Your Money, Your Sanity, and Our Planet

# About the Author

Pamela Beason is the author of the Sam Westin Mysteries, the Neema Mysteries, and the Run for Your Life Adventure Trilogy, as well as several romantic suspense and nonfiction books. She has received the Daphne du Maurier Award and two Chanticleer Book Reviews Grand Prizes for her writing, as well as an award from Library Journal and other romance and mystery awards. Pam is a former private investigator and freelance writer who lives in the Pacific Northwest, where she escapes into the wilderness whenever she can to hike and kayak and scuba dive.

http://pamelabeason.com

Made in the USA
San Bernardino, CA
26 March 2020

66387593R00141